Keith Dixon was born in Yorkshire and grew up in the Midlands. He's been writing since he was thirteen years old in a number of different genres: thriller, espionage, science fiction, literary.

He's the author of eight novels in the Sam Dyke Investigations series, three in the Paul Storey Thriller series and two other non-crime works, as well as two collections of blog posts on the craft of writing.

When he's not writing he enjoys reading, learning the guitar, watching movies and binge-inhaling great TV series.

He's currently spending more time in France than is probably good for him.

THE PRIVATE LIE

KEITH DIXON

A Sam Dyke Investigation

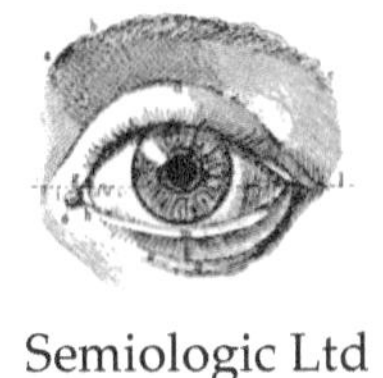

Semiologic Ltd

To Liz

CHAPTER ONE

I don't care how experienced you are as a private investigator, when your son is holding a heavyweight Desert Eagle pistol on you, and he's not smiling, it gets your attention.

'Is it loaded?' I said.

'No fun if it's not,' he said.

I considered my options. I could rush him—but my desk was between us. I could sweet-talk him—but I wasn't in the mood and I didn't think he was, either.

'You've got a plan to get away,' I said.

'Not that you'd notice. I'm as shocked as you are to get this far.' Coming as it did from a skinny teenager's body, his voice was surprisingly confident and strong.

'You need a plan if you're going to shoot someone,' I said. 'I don't think you've thought this through.'

'If I'd have thought this through I wouldn't have come. I had to do it like on impulse.'

'Impulsiveness isn't a good trait in someone holding a gun.'

'And being mouthy isn't good for someone staring down

its barrel.'

He had a point. I watched his eyes and gauged his breathing. There was no hand-shake and he hadn't cracked a sweat. Two minutes previously I'd been browsing through a copy of Uncut magazine when he'd knocked and entered without invitation. A slim youth with dark hair wearing a green hooded anorak over pale washed jeans and scuffed Nike trainers. He'd checked that I was Sam Dyke, private investigator of this parish, then reached inside his anorak and pulled out the gun like an archaeologist with a rare find, holding it carefully but just tight enough to be secure. In that confident voice he'd told me his name was Dan and asked whether I knew who he was. He was surprised when I said I did.

Now he asked, 'Don't you want to know why I'm here?' He waved the gun slightly, as though it might encourage curiosity.

'You'll tell me eventually. I'm more interested in how you found me.'

'Never mind how,' he said. 'The point is, I'm here and you're there.'

I crossed my arms and he took a step backwards.

'Go steady,' he said.

My office is square, with one door and one window looking out over the centre of Crewe, and holds a desk, a leather seat for me and two upright chairs for clients.

I'd never had more than two clients in my office at one time. I didn't think I could take the excitement.

'So let me get this straight,' I said. 'I'm guessing you found out I'm your dad and you think I'm responsible for your mother's death. You've never met either of us and inside five minutes of tracking me down, you're willing to kill me.'

For the first time I saw a cloud of doubt cross his face.

'Who said anything about killing you?' he asked.

I nodded at the gun. 'Unless I'm mistaken, that's not the new Nokia you're pointing at me.'

He looked at the handgun and was quiet for a moment. Then he said, 'You're just like I thought you'd be.'

'How's that, then?'

'Cocky Yorkshireman. Showing how tough you are. Not really interested in me and what I'm doing here. Nice to meet you, Dad.'

'Take a seat and we'll chat. How does a nice cup of tea sound?'

'Don't take the piss.'

'Then how about telling me what you want before your gun arm gets tired and you shoot me by accident? You're beginning to look sleepy.'

This time he didn't say anything but pulled up one of the client chairs and sat in it, dropping his slight frame as if he were no more than bones wrapped in clothing. He looked around at the office briefly.

'So this is where you make a living,' he said. 'What is it that private investigators do nowadays? Serve court papers? Photograph adulterers?'

'You're talking top-of-the-range work there.'

'I looked you up on the internet. You don't exist, do you? No web presence at all. Probably just as well. The sites I did see were a joke—lots of photos of middle-aged white men trying to look trustworthy while wearing a suit and tie.'

'We meet down the golf club and regale each other with stories about our wacky clients.'

The April rain suddenly threw itself against my office window and we both looked at it.

'So where are we, then?' I asked.

'I'm thinking,' he said. 'I'm beginning to wonder whether you're up to it.'

'Up to what?'

'I want you to help me,' he said. 'There's this girl, Kelly. We were going out but she dumped me a couple of months ago.'

'Am I to blame for that as well?'

'Shut up and listen. We were living in a squat and then all of a sudden she's gone. We'd been together for like six months and she didn't even leave me a note. That's why I'm thinking something's not right. She didn't tell anybody where she was going. No sign of her anywhere. Then someone I know told me she was in Manchester and saying she wasn't coming back.'

'Who's this someone?'

'You'll find out.'

'Okay. Does she work?'

He laughed. 'Not what you'd call a proper job. Not exactly on the executive career path. More like anything for money.'

'She got a habit?'

'Too many cigarettes. And she prefers a party to reading a book. Bad girl.'

I smiled grimly. 'Sounds like a prize catch for my son and heir.'

He looked away as if he were suddenly interested in the rain splattering my windows. His eyes looked impossibly hurt. I noticed that he had the long lashes of his mother. His dead mother. I felt a small stab of guilt in my chest but kept smiling at him. At least I think my expression was a smile.

'Yeah, well,' he said eventually. 'So your job is to help me find her.'

'I don't think so.'

'You owe me,' he said, his voice cold. 'You dumped my mother, you dumped me, you left me with people who had no interest in me except what I was worth for bringing in cash. I think a little help isn't too much to ask.'

'If you've done your research you know I had no idea you were alive. Your mother didn't tell me. Your foster parents didn't tell me. The little jiminy cricket who sits on my shoulder and looks after me didn't whisper in my ear and tell me. Now you're here I'm glad to meet you and have a conversation, but don't blame me for not doing something I wasn't aware I was supposed to do.'

'Like trying to find out anything about me?' He became agitated. 'My mother's been dead four months and I haven't heard a word from you. And don't tell me you didn't know about me because that's not true.' He pulled up short, a little breathless.

Now I knew who had told him – a woman I met when investigating a case a few months before. She was married to the man who murdered Tara, Dan's mother. As it turned out, I later killed her husband.

It had been a complicated affair.

'I don't think you understand how this stuff works,' I said. 'I do this for a living. People pay me money. I perform a service. I can't afford to take on charity cases, especially when the police would be your best bet in a situation like this.'

He raised the gun again. Its small black o came to rest on me. Looking down the barrel of a gun is always a religious experience – whatever your spiritual beliefs, it brings you quickly to faith.

'I don't think you understand,' he said. 'You don't have a choice.'

'What—you're going to follow me around for the next

few days pointing a gun at my head? It'll make bath-times difficult.'

'If you don't say yes I won't need the next few days.'

'Been reading your Greek tragedy, have you?'

'What?'

'Never mind. I read. The result of having too much time on my hands during stake-outs. Look, even if I help you find this girl—'

'Kelly.'

'—what if she doesn't want to come back? What if she was running away from you?'

'I've thought about that. I don't believe it, but if she says that's how it is, then OK. Just so she can tell me to my face. I want to know she's safe.'

I looked at him and felt sorry for him again. The need for reassurance lingered in his eyes like a memory he couldn't erase.

'I have a full case load,' I lied. 'I can't just drop everything because you're pointing a gun at me.'

'Can you think of a better reason?'

'People are expecting me to finish what I started. That might not mean anything to you, but it's my reputation at stake.'

'Think what your reputation will be if it gets out you refused to help your own son. And it *will* get out.'

We stared at each other across the desk while the rain beat against the window. I admired his persistence, maybe even recognised where it came from.

I raised a hand. 'OK, I'll help you find Kelly,' I said. 'But you and me have some serious talking to do. It sounds like people have been filling your head with shit for eighteen years. I don't like that.'

'Well perhaps you should have been there.'

'Perhaps I should have been an astronaut and flown to the moon. It was never going to happen. Now for God's sake put that toy down and let's go eat lunch.'

He turned the gun towards himself and looked down the barrel. He glanced at me, then slowly pulled the trigger until the firing pin made a plastic 'phut' sound.

He said, 'How could you tell?'

'That's why I'm the detective and you're not.'

I didn't tell him that had it been a real Desert Eagle, and loaded, he could never have held it trained on me for so long without wavering. It's too heavy.

You have to keep some detective secrets to yourself, otherwise everyone would have a licence and there wouldn't be enough work to go around.

CHAPTER TWO

We were sitting in my beat-up Cavalier outside Crewe railway station, avoiding the hard stares of the taxi drivers whose parking slots we were taking. I had the engine ticking over to keep the cabin warm. Travellers glanced briefly at us as they walked in or out of the sliding glass doors into the station. Once a busy hub of the rail network, it was gradually becoming more modernised — which seemed to mean fewer staff and more machines to do their work.

I watched Dan in the passenger seat. Every now and then I caught a look of his mother flickering across his face — a slightly bitter cast to his eyes as he noticed something and judged it in the same instant.

'When did he say he'd arrive?' I asked.

'He'll be here in a minute.'

'We've been waiting twenty. Why is he arriving at the train station if he lives here in Crewe?'

'Are you always this impatient? I thought you said you went on stake-outs and followed people and watched them for like days and days.'

'That's when I'm getting paid. It's called work.'

'He had family business in Yorkshire,' he said. 'Oh, but you wouldn't understand that, would you?'

He stared at me as though waiting for an argument, then turned round in his seat and looked back at the doors of the station. Another taxi blared its horn as it went past.

'You haven't told me anything about yourself,' I said. 'Tough life being a foster kid. Did they move you around much?'

He shrugged. 'Bit late for that, Dad. You had your chance and I'm not interested now.'

I said to Dan, 'You weren't listening when I told you your mother lied to me, were you?'

'Seems to me you gave up pretty easy. She scoots off to London and you didn't even follow her? Weren't you curious? Or angry?'

'Things were different then,' I said. 'I was barely twenty and I had no money. It wasn't so easy.'

'Oh, right. It was before trains and cars were invented. I was forgetting.'

'Your mother made it obvious she didn't want me coming after her. As far as I was concerned the marriage was over. She lied to me about the miscarriage and I supposed she felt guilty. Or angry. She didn't get in touch for eighteen years so how was I supposed to know different?'

'Happy families,' Dan said. I looked at his profile—I saw my straight nose and recognised in him the gawkiness I'd had when I was his age. Running and weights had changed my shape, but there'd been a time when I'd had his concave stomach and thin wrists.

I gave him a minute but he didn't ask about his mother. So far he didn't seem interested in her at all.

'So tell me about Kelly,' I said. 'You've hardly said

anything about her. How did you meet? How long had you been together? You know, the kind of stuff you'd normally tell your Dad.'

'Why should I tell you? All you need to know is what she looks like and I've given you a photograph.'

'Humour me.'

He turned away. 'What's to tell?' he said. 'She changes her mind all the time, about everything. Generally she wants what she can't have and vice versa. It's a fun relationship.'

'But you like her?'

'Who said so?'

'You've come a long way to find her. You've threatened me with a plastic gun. That must count for something.'

'Do you have to make jokes all the time?'

'It's my way of coping with the fundamental pain of human existence. How did you meet her?'

His eyes flicked towards me. 'In a crack den—where else do you think young people of today hang out?'

'You buying or selling?'

'Oh for God's sake,' he said. He turned around in his seat. Almost immediately he muttered, 'He's here,' and climbed out of the car.

The back door opened and within seconds a pungent smell of body odour entered the cabin. There was a crackling sound as the CDs I left on the rear seat were pushed carelessly to one side, and when I looked in the rear-view mirror I saw an elf looking back at me, a wide grin splitting his triangular face. 'Evenin', Dad,' he said. 'I'm John. Most people call me Pedlar John, which is OK by me.'

He sat back and spread his arms to rest them on top of the cracked and faded seat. 'Plush,' he said, apparently without irony.

Dan slammed the rear door and climbed in next to me.

'Let's go,' he said.

Pedlar John was the opposite of Dan. Where Dan was taciturn, John was curious and loud. Where Dan was dry, John was wide-eyed and naive. He seemed to have a desire to explain everything about himself. He maintained a running commentary as we headed north. The air in the cabin recovered some of its freshness as I changed the air-con to suck in new supplies from outside. I'd noticed that in contrast to Pedlar John, Dan smelled clean and his hair seemed washed.

Sam Dyke, beauty consultant.

When Pedlar John paused for breath, I asked, 'Where's the nickname come from?'

He seemed pleased, as though people rarely asked him questions. 'I have a little routine,' he said. 'When times are hard, I get me big bag out, get down to Poundstretcher and stock up on some cleaning gear, then get round on the knock. Got meself a fake plastic ID that I flash quicker than the eye can follow and flog the goods on the doorstep at twice what I paid for them.'

He caught my eye in the rear-view mirror. 'Lonely housewives,' he winked. 'Know what I mean?'

Dan laughed. I kept my eyes on the road.

Pedlar John had been scrabbling around in the back.

'Hey, Dad, you got a load of CDs but I don't know any of these bands. Who the hell are Whiskeytown? And Richmond Fontaine? Is this old shit or what?'

I took a deep breath and wondered whether it was worth my while educating a philistine in the wonders of American alternative music of the 1990s. The car was crammed with CDs that were rare or at least hard to get hold of unless you were willing to trawl the internet.

'Hey,' he said, 'I've heard of this guy. Ryan Adams. Like Country shit.'

'Keep your hands off the goods,' I said. 'If you don't like it you don't have to listen.'

'I didn't mean anything. Put one on—here, this one.'

He thrust Wilco's Being There into my lap. I picked it up and gave it to Dan. 'Put it on,' I said. I'd replaced the Cavalier's tape deck with a Blaupunkt CD player but I thought its clarity was going to be wasted on my passengers. After a moment the strange drum riff of Misunderstood and Jeff Tweedy's pained vocals filled the Cavalier's cabin. I caught Dan and Pedlar John glancing at each other behind my shoulder but couldn't tell what the look meant.

I focused on my driving and decided being a parent was too hard. I would definitely not do it again until I'd had proper training.

CHAPTER THREE

The dark sky was still squeezing out a grey rain when we arrived in Manchester and parked behind Piccadilly Gardens. Although it was only 4.15, lights were beginning to appear bright in the city centre. Commuters and other travellers on their way to the train station stepped around us, hunching their necks into their overcoats like turtles.

'Tell me again why we're here,' I said, brushing water off my leather jacket. You have to keep yourself neat if you're going to maintain the good reputation of private detection.

Dan looked exasperated. 'You're a bit slow on the uptake for someone who does this for a living,' he said.

'I've been threatened by a plastic gun and had my musical taste questioned by a pixie with BO,' I said. 'I'm sorry if I'm not catching all the nuances of our conversation.'

'Yeah, go easy,' Pedlar John said. 'He doesn't know what we know, does he?'

Dan sighed. 'I'll keep the story short, so you can remember it. Kelly and I were introduced to John in London a couple of months ago. He was visiting his friend, Billy, who we knew. The four of us hung out together for a week, then John got bored and came home, back up to Crewe. A few weeks later Kelly split, I didn't know where to.'

'Then I get a text message,' Pedlar John prompted.

'Yeah, one of Billy's mates had come up here to see United in a semi-final. So he was walking around town that night, after the match, and he bumps into Kelly outside Marks and Spencers. She barely says hello, then walks off. But not before giving him a good idea what she was up to. The next day, this bloke has a think about what he'd seen and texts John.'

'Why would he do that?' I asked. 'Why didn't he contact you?'

'Because he didn't have my number but he had John's.'

'So then *I* phoned Dan and let him know,' Pedlar John said, apparently pleased with himself.

'What *was* she up to?' I asked.

Dan said nothing but looked around at the street corners. I followed his gaze. I suddenly got it. We were in that part of Manchester they call Little Soho, where the working girls show up when the night clubs and hotels are doing their best evening trade.

'Great,' I said. 'So she's working the streets.'

Dan avoided my eyes. Pedlar John noticed this and spoke up.

'Dan knew you worked up here as an investigator. He hopped on a train and we did some investigating of our own and found your advert in the Yellow Pages.'

'I'm in Crewe. You're in Crewe. What a coincidence.'

He was unfazed. 'It's what makes the world go around.'

I looked at Dan. 'So why do you need me? You've done all right so far. You found which city she's in, and probably the streets she's walking. What do you think I can do that you can't do for yourself?'

He stared back at me.

'I can't do this alone,' he said. For the first time he seemed nervous.

I said, 'OK. Strange city, strange people, I can understand that.'

'Yeah,' Pedlar John said. 'It ain't easy.'

Dan glanced at him with a look I didn't think was completely approving. But he said nothing and turned his attention back to the streets.

I'd always rather do something than talk about it, and more conversation at this stage seemed pointless. I said, 'So we are where we are. What's the plan now?'

Dan said, 'If she's working the streets she's probably got someone looking after her. Isn't that what happens? John knows a couple of people we can ask questions of.'

'So I'm just the chauffeur to get you here.'

'If you want to go home, do it.'

'What, and have you barge into my office brandishing a shotgun tomorrow morning?'

Pedlar John stared at Dan admiringly. 'So you did it then?' he said. 'Good on you, mate. Didn't think you had the balls.'

Looking at him, I saw that Dan's friend was older than I'd first thought. He was probably in his mid- to late twenties. I didn't like the way he'd been instrumental in getting Dan involved in all this. I didn't like his cockiness. And I didn't like the fact that he was leading this fishing expedition. I thought I'd keep an eye on him. He was way too slippery.

'So are you coming or not?' Dan asked me. 'You can wait in the car if you want.'

'If we're going to do something, let's do it.'

'You're on,' John said, and set off at a brisk trot.

Dan and I fell in behind him as he crossed the road and headed towards the railway station. He wore a baggy woollen jumper and carried a denim tote-bag. It was like following a mediaeval jester on the way to court, before he'd put on the cap and bells and attached the balloon to his stick.

Dan ran ahead of me as though he didn't want to be seen with an old geezer who might have been taken for his dad.

We turned down a murky side street and Pedlar John dived into a bookshop, leaving its door bell tinkling like an aftershock. Dan and I followed him into the darkness. The smell of yellowing, musty paper hit me at once. It was the kind of bookshop which sold second-hand paperbacks and old cinema magazines and, if you asked, you might be let into a curtained area at the back of the establishment where your earthier appetites would be looked after. For some reason, these shops always flourished around train stations. Perhaps in earlier times they were a respite for commercial travellers in search of entertainment for their overnight stops. In the age of the Internet I didn't think such places were still viable, but I was obviously wrong.

Having hurtled into the shop, Pedlar John had come to a halt and was looking with academic loftiness at a book that was splayed open on a table. A sign marked 'Sale!' written in marker pen on red card was tacked to one end of the table. Pedlar John turned over a leaf of the book as though considering the quality of its typeface and the weave of its paper. Dan moved over to browse through a case of science fiction paperbacks. I stood inside the door and looked around, noticing the beaded curtain behind the sales desk, counting the number of vertical stacks—three—and seeing that we were the only customers in the shop.

Eventually Pedlar John moved from the Sale table and went to talk to the assistant, a grizzled, overweight man wearing a stained tee-shirt who had come through the bead curtain and stood watching us with passive disdain. As John spoke, the man listened without expression, then turned and went back through the curtain, which rustled chaotically. After a short while a black man six inches taller and a stone heavier than me came out and immediately pointed a finger at John.

'You,' he said. 'Fuck off out of here unless you want your bollocks for ear-rings.'

John put his hands up. 'Sparkle, mate, I'm innocent. Just trying to find someone, gangsta.'

The black man came round the counter, muscles first. His arms were thick under a yellow silk shirt. He had the look of someone who used to fight but had lost too many times. His face was large and his eyes showed red in the corners. 'I tole you before if you come 'round here I'd do you. You deaf or what?' He poked Pedlar John in the chest with a stiff ebony finger, then looked up as he saw me approaching. 'What you want, mister?'

'I want you to leave him alone,' I said. 'That's for starters.'

He stood tall and looked down at me. He smelled of cigarettes and a sweet deodorant. 'Yeah, and what's for followers?'

'We need to ask some questions, if that's all right.'

He looked around and saw only the three of us in the shop. Then his face split in a grin. 'You can ask, but you get no answers.'

'That's not a very nice attitude.'

'Who needs nice?' he asked. 'And who the fuck are you to talk to me like that?'

I saw his mass shift before he raised his arm, so I was

prepared when his fist came up. I'd been ready for this as soon as I saw him point his finger at John. I leaned to one side to avoid his fist, and while he was off-balance I short-punched him on the nose and stamped on his foot for good measure. I felt a bone give under my heel. He doubled over and raised his hands to his face at the same time. Blood started to trickle through his fingers. The assistant went pale and took a step back from the counter.

'Wow,' Pedlar John said.

Through his fingers, Sparkle said, 'Why'd you do that, man?'

'I told you, you weren't being very nice.'

'You've busted my nose.'

'It'll mend. It might teach you some manners.'

'It's my job, man, keep the punters in place. You shouldn't have done that. Gonna have to report you.'

'Do what you want,' I said. 'Do you know anything about a girl called Kelly?'

'Yeah, she's my girlfriend.' He spat blood on to the floor and looked up at me. 'Who the fuck's Kelly?'

'Keep saying you don't know her,' I said. 'I hope for your sake you're right.'

I nodded at Dan and Pedlar John to leave the shop, then followed them. They were standing on the wet pavement looking at me as I closed the door.

'What?' I said.

'Good work,' Dan said. 'You've only gone and pissed off one of the biggest crime families in the North West. I'm glad we brought you along to help out.'

CHAPTER FOUR

The traffic processed slowly out of Manchester, crawling along Princess Parkway and finally speeding up as it hit the broader reaches of the M56.

Dan and Pedlar John had thrown themselves into the back seat and now peered from a window each at the passing headlights and road signs. We'd said next to nothing since we'd stared at each other on the pavement outside the bookshop. The knuckles of my right hand were bruised where I'd caught Sparkle on his big nose and my ego was bruised even more by the thought that I'd dived straight in without considering the consequences. What had I been doing? Showing off for the youngsters? Protecting the brood? Acting out the irritation I was feeling with the whole exercise?

Pedlar John broke the silence. 'We only needed to ask a couple of questions,' he said. 'Now we're really in the shit. If Sparkle says anything to the Twins, we're screwed.'

'Who are the Twins?' I asked.

'The bad guys,' Dan said. 'The Wilder boys. Little Jimmy

and Pete Wilder. The ones we've been trying to avoid.'

'By poking around in their business? Good tactic.'

Pedlar John lifted his head from the glass and leaned forward. 'You don't understand, Dad. The Ginger Twins are Liverpool. They've only just moved into Manchester. They've bought that shop and one or two other places. Camouflage. An excuse to come into town. Get away from the Docks. They've also bought Sparkle, big fucker that he is. I thought he might know Kelly. I didn't expect you to come over all Mike Tyson.'

'Where does Sparkle fit in?'

'Used to run women for himself but it was like a package deal. The Twins showed him how it would be to his advantage to work for them and give them a cut. Everyone wins.' He leaned back again. 'Little Jimmy's a mean fucker. I wouldn't have liked to be in the room when they were negotiating with Sparkle. No wonder he wanted to pop me. He's been wound up like a toy soldier, poor bastard. He won't want to answer to Jimmy.'

I realised that my hands were tight on the steering wheel and loosened them before I steered us into a ditch.

'Let me get this straight,' I said. 'You've had us walk into the middle of some kind of gang war just to find a tart who's not phoned home?'

'Yes,' Dan said. 'She's just a tart and you're the big-headed bastard who's lit up our names in lights so they know who we are and probably where to get hold of us.'

I found Pedlar John's face in the mirror. 'They know who you are?'

'I've had dealings, yeah. That's why I steer clear of Liverpool now.'

'What did you do?'

'Nothing. They thought I was selling stuff on their patch

and they wanted a cut. It wasn't anything.'

'"Stuff"?'

'Nothing hard. Everyone knows Jimmy doesn't tolerate that so I steered clear. Just a bit of weed occasionally.'

I took a deep breath.

'And would they know Dan?' I asked.

'Not necessarily. Look, man, don't blame me. I was only doing what my mate Dan wanted me to do. I told him it was risky messing about with these boys. It's not my fault you're Prince bloody Charming.'

'He would have knocked your block off.'

'Not Sparkle. He's lost it. He's all bluster now and pointy fingers, but he never carries through. Damaged goods.'

'Why do you call them the Ginger Twins?'

Pedlar John snorted. 'Well there's the obvious. Irish carrot tops, the pair of them. Used to be like identical, but Little Jimmy's built himself up a bit. Pete too, but not as much. Little Jimmy's like a walking chemists. Steroid city. He always wears black tee-shirts and Pete wears white ones. Used to be how you could tell them apart. Now Little Jimmy's big as a fucking house so you can't really miss him.'

'Sound like fine upstanding citizens.'

'Then there's the other reason,' Pedlar John went on.

'What's that?'

'They've got the ginger hair right enough, cut short. But the story goes they like to ginger you up. Know what I mean? If you work for them and they don't like how things are going, Little Jimmy gets his snippers out. Gardening things, what do you call them—'

'Secateurs.'

'That's them. He snips people's fingers off, the weird bastard. Takes revenge into his own hands, you might say.'

I saw that Dan was looking at Pedlar John with his eyes

widening. I was glad to see that he didn't find it as amusing as his friend did.

I said, 'We've got to get one thing straight. If we're carrying on with this—and I'm not saying we are—then you've got to tell me everything you know. I can't go around with one hand tied behind my back.'

'What do you mean, "If we're carrying on with this"?' Dan said. 'Are you chickening out?'

'I can't let amateurs like you get caught up in this kind of stuff,' I said.

Dan looked away. 'Jesus, I don't believe this. You're an arrogant bastard, aren't you?'

'I've been doing this kind of thing a long time. You know when to stick and when to twist.'

'And when to run away with your tail between your legs.'

The air in the cabin was cold. I turned up the heater and opened a window to help the windscreen de-mist. The hissing sound of traffic on wet road occupied us all for a while.

Eventually I said, 'Finding Kelly if someone doesn't want her found is going to be difficult. It might have been easier to set up surveillance on where she worked to see if she turned up again. By talking to that Sparkle guy, what you've done is set alarm bells ringing. If Kelly is here and the bad guys are putting her to work for them, which seems likely, then they'll find out we're looking. Prostitution is a thriving market, and people talk. The gangs treat it like a slave trade. They auction women off to each other in pubs.'

I looked at Dan. 'You think I'm kidding? Read the papers. The coppers can't keep up, it's so prevalent. Only it's Eastern European women who go under the hammer these days, not Africans. We could have gone about this differently if I'd known more.'

'Or if you'd kept your hands in your pockets,' Dan muttered.

No one said anything else till we arrived back in Crewe.

CHAPTER FIVE

I dropped Dan and Pedlar John outside the house they were sharing. It was a large terraced three-storey job in the centre of Crewe. As I drove away they were leaning into the front door to force it open. I guess they didn't have a key.

I let myself into my own house and turned on all the downstairs lights. I'd recently fitted some patio doors at the back. Now I could see over the fields that fell away to the trees that hid the council houses beyond and the school playing fields that I ran across most mornings. But at this time of night all I could see was my own reflection holding a can of Heineken at port arms.

I drank half the can then boiled water in the kettle for pasta. While the kettle grumbled I phoned my last remaining friend where I'd worked in C E, Dickie Baines, and asked him about the Ginger Twins.

'Jesus, Sam, get some clear water between you and them,' he said. 'Sack the client, move to Aberdeen and change your name.'

'That bad, eh?'

'If not worse.'

Dickie told me that the Twins had established their rep in the early nineties through a succession of roaring fights and gangland rucks in Liverpool, creating a small universe around them that consisted of distinct business empires in the building trade, tobacco smuggling, prostitution and, these days, online pornography routed through a host in the Pacific Islands. Each empire in this universe was actually a moral and ethical black hole in which thuggery, beatings, terrorism and robbery were legitimate business tactics. And the Ginger Twins were at the gravitational centre, sucking in the money and spewing out violence.

This didn't stop them following the traditional pattern of criminals in early middle-age, however—craving respectability. They owned houses a couple of streets from each other on the Wirral and ran building companies that tendered for both private and public business up and down the North West region. What's more, they'd stayed clean enough on the surface to be relatively successful with these tenders.

'So with all this going on,' I said, 'Why have they bought a dirty bookshop in Manchester?'

'Ah,' Dickie said. 'New developments. They've done Liverpool and they're spreading their tentacles like the grubby animals they are.'

'So it's a territory war, as per usual?'

'Well, Sam, they're a bit like you. Low boredom threshold. Soon as they've got the hang of something they have to move on. How is the world of private dicking, anyway? Is it full of sex and intrigue?'

'Half right,' I said.

'Let me guess—you're fighting the women off with both hands because of your dark good looks and exciting job description.'

'What else should I know about Little Jimmy and Pete?'

'Other than that they're crazy Irish bastards who never grew up and think the world owes them a living? Nothing much.'

'Have you got an address for them?'

Dickie's laugh was hollow. 'Don't tell me—you're going to ask them a few sensible questions.'

'While holding my hand over my crotch.'

He laughed. 'I'll email you. I don't have them here.'

'Thanks.'

He said, 'Don't thank me. Make sure you've got the name of a good dentist before you knock on their door.'

I hung up.

There was a rattle at the front door and Laura came in. She looked pink and flustered, but her casual elegance reasserted itself as soon as she put down a large bag of shopping. A brisk run of her hands down her front, a shake of her straw-coloured hair, and she was herself again, slim and sleek, and with enough sex appeal to keep my eyes glued to her whatever she did.

A couple of months ago she'd started a new job in Nantwich, which meant her office was halfway between her house and mine. As a result we avoided the Big Discussion as to whether one of us moved in with the other. Four months on and I still looked forward to her arrival every night—and if she decided she was going to spend the night in her own house, I sulked. Maybe I'd feel different after five months but I didn't think so.

'Are you ready to cook?' she asked briskly, starting to unpack the shopping. 'I could eat several horses.'

I helped her with the bags. 'Good day?'

She gave me a pitying look, then offered puckered lips for

a kiss, which I took. At my age you accept romance wherever you can find it.

'Don't give me a hard time tonight,' she said, finally uncovering the tomatoes and the mince and clearing a place to start preparation. She'd moved from marketing into PR, a change of disciplines whose gradations of difference I was plainly too coarse to understand. All I knew was that her work now intruded further into our life than before.

'Is this the new client?' I asked. I had concentrated long enough to remember some key points.

'Bloomfield the Bastard, we're calling him. Takes twice as long to make up his mind as anyone else, then changes it anyway. Sorry I'm late. What have you been up to?'

In relation to Dan this was my first test of the evening. I failed it by changing the subject: 'Want a drink?'

'Gin, please. Good, you've boiled the kettle.'

I put ice in two glasses then left the kitchen and went through to where I kept the gin. Laura knew about Dan, but like me she'd never met him. I wasn't sure I was able to talk about what had happened today just yet. Especially as I was still feeling raw from the way it had turned out. Laura preferred safety and a certain amount of predictability, which often made my life seem edgier and more dangerous than I felt it really was. Telling her that Dan had turned up on my doorstep pointing a gun at me, and that we'd set off fireworks in Manchester, would raise her protective hackles while at the same time releasing a rats' cage of worries that would follow her around for days on end, turning her into an unwilling Pied Piper who couldn't shake off the products of her own imagination.

She looked up from the chopping board as I went back into the kitchen and found lemon to slice. 'Well?' she said. 'Another exciting day preventing international bank fraud?'

'Something came up,' I said glibly. 'Ended up in Manchester this afternoon. Got wet.'

'Interesting case?'

'Not sure yet. See how it goes.'

I handed her the drink then backed out of the kitchen feeling slightly unclean. I didn't want to lie to her but it had come more easily than I liked.

Laura went to bed after the ten o'clock news but I was too wired and stayed up for another hour reading Stephen Ambrose's *D-Day*. The scenes it conjured in my head didn't help my frame of mind. Later I crept up the stairs and got into bed quietly. Laura stirred but didn't wake, the S-curve of her back undulating like a distant sea disturbed in its troubled depths by the violent passions of unseen monsters.

I lay on my back and stared at the ceiling, going over and over in my mind's eye the first ever day that I'd spent with my son.

CHAPTER SIX

Little Jimmy looked sideways at Pete, driving the Merc one-handed as if he were Schumacher, the lord of all he surveyed. He always had to look cool and in control. He couldn't bear to have you think he might not be in charge, Jimmy thought. That's what he always wanted to be—the boss. Ever since they'd been young, Pete had been the one with the ideas and the drive. They were identical physically and in most other ways. But Pete had something extra—ambition. He always wanted to win. He couldn't stand coming second.

Jimmy looked through the side window at the passing streets. Liverpool was slowly crumbling away. The fabric of the houses and the roads was pock-marked and brittle, like chalk cliffs on the point of collapse. Mile after mile of grey terraces slipped past the Mercedes' window, each block of houses replaced by an identical block, each house painted a drab cream or brown, each garden a tangled mess of weeds and concrete.

'Fuck's a matter with you?' Pete demanded.

Jimmy said nothing and popped a breath mint. Sometimes he just didn't fancy talking, especially when Pete was on his case.

Pete carried on anyway.

'Have you done what we talked about?

'I'll do it when I've got time.'

'You'll do it in the next week.'

'Fuck you.'

'Fuck you too,' Pete said. 'What are your plans, exactly? Keep her locked up till she agrees to marry you? Gonna walk her down the aisle with a big bunch of roses and a honeymoon in Blackpool?'

'None of your business.'

'My business if it fucks up this deal.'

'It won't.'

'Too fuckin true it won't. I'll top her myself before then.'

Jimmy said, 'You leave her alone. I'm lookin after her.'

'I can tell. Keepin her locked up like an hamster. Got her a big wheel, too, 'ave you?'

'Go home to your own missus, if you can stand it. Dried up prune, she is.'

'Watch your mouth.'

'No, don't like talking about yours, do you? Too busy sticking your nose in other people's business.'

Pete looked straight ahead through the windscreen, a muscle working in his cheek.

'Just watch what you're doing with her. There's too much hanging on this for me to be thinking about some trollop you're saving for a rainy day.'

The site was empty. They walked on the planks that crossed the muddy ground and went up the steps into the Portakabin. Pete had the key and he looked around before opening up. That was him—always secretive. Always worried about what might happen if it went wrong. Jimmy followed him inside and shut the door.

'Fuckin cold in here,' he said.

'Put a jumper on.'

They grinned at each other—that was their mother's saying whenever the gas meter ran out and they didn't have any money.

'Get 'er going,' Pete said, and Jimmy pushed past him into the cubicle at the back. He unlocked the cabinet and took out the laptop. Pete didn't want it kept in either of their houses, just in case. Jimmy booted it up and ran the Automatic Identification System software. Every ship over 300 tons was required to broadcast its location, speed, status and other information. This information was picked up by different tracking systems worldwide and made available to interested parties, usually for a fee. Jimmy had felt really cool when he learned this. Something he could do that his brother couldn't. He zoomed into a section of the ocean north of Africa.

'Where is it now?' Pete asked.

Jimmy hunted down the green triangle representing The Madrigal, their ship.

'South of the Scilly Isles.'

'How far's that, then?'

'Still on time. Weather's not been bad.'

'Still plenty of time for that to happen,' Pete said.

'You're such a tosser—always worrying.'

'That's because you're such a stupid prick. I've always had to look after you.'

Jimmy shook his head. 'Here we go.'

'Wipe your snotty nose and pull your trousers up, that's all I've ever done.'

'Makes me wonder how I ever manage to have a life.'

'Well you don't, do you? Unless you count staring at a screen playing your X-Box having a life.'

'We done here?'

Pete nodded. 'We don't need anything to go wrong with this.'

'I know.'

'Lot of planning and dosh gone into it.'

'I was there, Pete. You don't have to tell me.'

'Just saying. You've got to be focused. Not arsing around like usual.'

Little Jimmy closed down the software and went through the sequence to shut down the computer. He didn't like it when Pete had a go at him because he was partly right. He'd painted himself into a corner. He had no friends—no one he could trust, anyway—and he didn't really like the people he worked with. What he had was a plan, though. It was in the film. Old film from the sixties. There was this man who was no good with girls, but he came into a ton of money. Won the pools or something. Then he got himself a place that was shut off from the outside world. Like a basement. And he collected girls. In the film he collected this posh tart and kept her locked up. He wanted her to see him for what he really was, then she'd fall in love with him. It ended badly in the film, but it didn't have to. Little Jimmy still liked the idea.

It was something he could work with.

CHAPTER SEVEN

The sun was low as I parked and pushed through shoppers towards Piccadilly Gardens. The season was turning, the air warmer each day. It was too early for any real action so I found a coffee shop and drank two lattes while reading more of Ambrose's *D-Day*. The heroics on the beach were just starting. Those who had made it were huddled under the cliff-face wondering what they were going to do with all their weapons and radio gear under water. When the waitress behind the counter started giving me evil looks I ordered a toasted ham pannini to buy me another hour's inattention.

The clientele morphed from shoppers drinking tea before catching the tram or bus home, to early-evening sophisticates downing a pre-club glass of wine. I began to feel out of place in my denim shirt and leather jacket—I should have been wearing a nice Gap shirt, slimline Italian trousers with bootcut bottoms and perhaps a pair of clean Nike trainers. And I should have been twenty-one with a line in patter for the ladeez, a job in new media and an Audi TT soft-top parked around the corner. No doubt my life would have seemed complete. I sighed and went back to my book.

When it began to turn dark I went outside and began searching. After a while my eyes tuned in—the girl who walked a little too slowly; the girl who stood smoking in a doorway; the girl who stood on the corner talking into a mobile phone.

I walked up to a teenaged girl wearing a thin green jacket with a floral pattern. She looked me up and down as though assessing me for threat. I said, 'Do you know a girl called Kelly?'

She turned away. 'Fuck off.'

'So you know her.'

'You buying or what?'

'I'm not buying.'

'Then I'm not talking. Never heard of her.'

She walked off.

The second girl turned away before I even got near. Maybe she thought I was a cop.

The third girl I talked to was younger than the others and more edgy. She smoked a Dunhill out of the corner of her mouth as if trying to keep the smoke from her eyes. She wore a short leather jacket and her hair was pulled back in a pony tail. Her skirt rose way above the knee, revealing plenty of dark stocking. When she lifted her face to me I saw she had bruised semi-circles under her eyes.

I asked my question.

'What's it to you?' she said.

'A friend is worried about her.'

She stopped pacing and looked me up and down. 'A friend?'

'Not me. Really. A friend. She's gone missing.'

'Not surprised.'

'Why?'

'Mixing with that crowd.'

'Who?

'Those yobs from Liverpool. Loudmouthed pumped-up arseholes.'

'Do you know their names?'

'Yeah—everyone knows who they are. Ginger nuts.'

'What happened?'

'Why should I say anything to you? You could be anyone.'

I showed her a twenty pound note.

She said, 'You're cheap, ain't you?'

She looked at it with disdain, then took it and pulled me into the shadows.

'Who are you?' she asked.

'Someone who's looking for her. What can you tell me?'

She hesitated, then shrugged. 'We were at a party, out in the country. Three or four of us. A bloke in a flash car come along and took us all. It was night, so I don't know where it was. Big house. Iron gates and all. We had a bit to drink in the car so by the time we got there we were up for anything.'

'Kelly was with you.'

'She was more nervous than me, which was a fucking miracle. I don't think she was really into it. I don't know her that much but I don't think she needs this shit.'

'What, like an amateur?'

'Don't get me wrong, she took the money same as the rest of us. But she was always like one step back.'

'What happened?'

'We arrived at this big house and the party had already started. Lots of thugs there. We were the entertainment, only Kelly was snapped up quick. Big bloke. I mean shit-house big. Black tee-shirt, shaved head. You could still tell he was a ginger, though. Eyebrows give him away.'

'He took her off?'

'Couldn't say. I just saw her with him and then I didn't see them any more. She wasn't in the car on the way back and I haven't seen her since.'

'Have you got any way of getting in touch with her?'

She reached into her purse and pulled out a business card. 'We give each other these, just in case,' she said.

I looked at it. There was just Kelly's name and a telephone number on it.

'What's your name?'

'Sophie. That's what they call me round here, anyway.'

I gave her one of my cards. 'Thanks, Sophie. I'd get out of this business if I were you.'

'Well you ent me, are you? What the fuck do you know?'

'Nothing.'

She stared at me. 'Well at least you're not like the other tossers who'd want something for the dosh.'

'Can I give you a lift anywhere?'

'Serious?'

I nodded. She thought for a moment then shook her head. 'I've got to put in some time tonight. The boss won't like it if I bunk off just yet.'

I shrugged and walked away. I didn't feel like being Galahad tonight. Then I stopped and turned back. Maybe I should give her some more money.

But she was gone.

I thought how easy it had been to find out what had happened to Kelly, and wondered why no one else seemed to have made the effort. I switched on my mobile and called the number on Kelly's card. It rang for a long time, then a man's voice came on the line. 'International Couriers.'

'Can I speak to Kelly?' I said.

'Give me your number and I'll call right back.'

'No thanks,' I said, and disconnected.

Very curious. The voice had an American accent. So who had I been talking to?

I walked back towards my car. The pavements were still busy and the traffic constant. After a moment I stepped into a doorway and watched people going by. When I stepped out again, Pedlar John was so surprised he lifted his hands towards his face as if to protect himself.

'Fuck!' he said, before remembering. 'Sorry, sorry, Mr Dyke. Good to see you.'

'Are you following me?'

'What—you mean this coincidence?'

'Is that what it is?'

'Course it is. Why would I follow you?'

'Usually I follow people to find out what they're up to.'

'Right—and I know what you're up to, don't I, looking for Kelly, right? You told us last night.'

I looked at him. There must have been something in my expression that made him want to talk. I find that happens quite a lot.

He said, 'I know some people here, right? I used to live in Manchester and this was my patch. I've still got friends, contacts, you know, people who might tell me stuff.'

'What are you doing with Dan?'

'How do you mean?'

'He's a youngster. You must have ten years on him. Why are you hanging around with him?'

His eyes became harder. 'I think you've got that wrong, Mr Dyke. I might not seem salubrious-like to you at the moment, but actually Dan's hanging around with me. That's my place we're in. It was Dan that came looking for me, not the other way round.'

He saw that it wasn't enough. 'And to be honest he reminds me a bit of myself, when I was his age. Idealistic. Wanting to do good. Wanting people to get on with each other. I've had to toughen up, Mr Dyke. I can help him.'

'I don't want you helping Dan more than you have to.'

'Right, that's a father's job.'

He didn't flinch as I took a step towards him. The little so-and-so had courage.

'Watch your step,' I said. 'If you do anything to hurt Dan you'll have me to answer to.'

He shrugged. 'You say so. Can I cadge a lift home?'

We said nothing on the journey back to Crewe. I put on Springsteen to drown out any conversation he wanted to make. When I dropped him off he turned in his seat before climbing out.

'These twins, Mr Dyke. You've got to watch out for them. From what I've seen they're real rough 'uns. Particularly Little Jimmy. You don't want to cross him.'

'Is that what you've seen?'

'They've got a reputation.'

'In my line of work I'm sure I've dealt with worse,' I said.

'I hope that's right,' he said. 'Otherwise you might have to raise your game.'

CHAPTER EIGHT

The next morning I got up early again and went for another run. When I finished I went straight into the large garage where I keep my gym equipment and did half an hour's weights. I did a series of jump shrugs and hang pulls to pump blood into my upper body, then ten overhead squats, the barbell held above me with stiff arms, to put some tension into my thighs. I needed to sweat and feel that my body was ready for anything, because today was going to be risky.

I made eggs and bacon with a little fried bread and drank half a carton of orange juice, then I made up sandwiches with ham and cheese and pickle, and brewed a thermos of tea. I also took some energy drinks from the back of the fridge and put them into a cool bag along with the sandwiches. Then I programmed the address that Dickie Baines had emailed me into my GPS and drove north again, towards the Wirral, the thumb of land that sticks out into the Irish sea between Liverpool and North Wales. The GPS took me across country, through Nantwich and Chester, till I hit the flat land that levelled out where the Irish Sea just made itself visible as a low wall of grey across the estuary.

Ness was a small village with large houses hidden behind walls and hedges that were neatly trimmed and shaped. I found Little Jimmy's house and parked a hundred yards up the road. Two brick pillars were connected by a large black gate, through which I could make out a complicated house with a couple of gable roofs, a large double garage, a gravelled drive with fountain, and louvered blinds on all the windows. I couldn't see in, but it was possible they could see out, especially as there was a security camera fixed to one of the brick pillars and another one mounted high on the wall over the front porch, which was also gabled. I guessed that Little Jimmy, as a builder, had constructed this himself to his own design. I reckoned he'd seen The Godfather too many times.

After an hour I'd eaten all the sandwiches and drunk all the drink, and it was barely midday. I'd seen no one enter or leave the house, and the only action I'd witnessed at all was a local resident walking a highly-pedigreed Afghan hound. I couldn't tell which was the more stuck up, dog or owner.

At about three o'clock a parcel was delivered to the house. The delivery man pressed a button on the left hand brick pillar and after a conversation and a wait of a few minutes, a goon came to the gate, unlatched it twelve inches, and signed for the package. It looked like three or four books in height and width, though from what I knew of crooks like him, I couldn't imagine Little Jimmy reading anything other than comics.

An hour later, the same goon came through the gates and walked down the road. He wore jeans and a black tee-shirt, with a short leather coat keeping off the afternoon chill. He walked with a slight roll, as though his thighs were too massive to move backwards and forwards and had to take a roundabout route.

Twenty minutes later he came back with a pint of milk and a newspaper. Even master criminals have basic needs. I kept low in the Cavalier and if he saw me he gave no sign.

Which was very clever of him, because five minutes later my door was suddenly yanked open and two large hairy hands pulled me out of my seat. I was face to face with the same goon. He was as big as me, had a close crop cut and pale skin that showed a deep scar running from the edge of his the nose down to his jaw. He held me by my lapels and pulled me to him.

'Having a good look, are we?' he said. 'Plenty to see, is there?'

'I'm sorry, do I know you?'

'Let's find out,' he said, and turned me towards the house. I noticed for the first time that he had a workmate with him, a younger man with bad skin who stood a couple of feet away shifting his weight from side to side as though unsure which pose to adopt. He needed to read his Goon's Manual if he was to go any further in this trade.

They took me through the iron gates. A new red Corvette squatted in front of the double garage, crouched for action. The front door opened as we approached and Little Jimmy stood there massively, looking like a plastic doll inflated to super-hero proportions in the arms, chest and thighs. He wore a black tee-shirt that struggled to contain his upper musculature, and green cargo pants which bulged in the thigh as though packed with telephone directories. His hair was close-cropped but visible—he hadn't gone for the full hardman bullet-head look. Perhaps there was some sense of identity wrapped up in the ginger hair that he couldn't dispose of entirely.

His smile was mean and cold eyed as he stood back and opened the door further. 'Well done, Mikey. Well spotted. Just bring him through to the kitchen.'

His accent was full Liverpool, the guttural, sing-song melody that was light in tone but faintly sarcastic in every word.

Mikey and the other man gripped my upper arms more tightly and led me through the house. We went from the tiled entrance hall, past a cloakroom and entered a large modern kitchen with an expanse of black granite worktop and white units lining three of the four walls. The fourth was largely taken up by tall windows that looked on to a neat garden where tidy shrubs and a perfect green lawn were visible. The single door in the wall of windows was closed. Its top half was also glass, so the view was unrestricted.

'Stop a second, lads,' Jimmy said.

The pain of his fist striking my stomach was more shocking because I wasn't ready for it. I felt bile rise in the back of my throat and worked hard to swallow it.

'You're a big feller,' he said, 'but I'm bigger than most so let's not have any mucking about. Who are you and why are you watching me?'

I panted for breath. 'I like your colour scheme. I was going to ask for some swatches.'

The second blow was even more disabling. After I doubled over I found I couldn't stand upright for, oh, a couple of centuries.

'You don't have to talk right now,' Little Jimmy said. 'You can save it for later, after we've got to know each other. Okay, lads, put him down.'

They let go of me and I sagged, but they'd placed a stool to catch me. I leaned over with my head down and calculated my chances of taking all three of them. Not very high.

'Saw you looking at the car,' he said conversationally. 'The dog's bollocks, ain't it? Only had it a few days. Goes like shit off a shovel.'

'You know what they say about men with big red cars,' I gasped.

'Yeah, they've got a lot of money. Not like your pokey little ... What is it, Cavalier?'

'First prize.'

'I'm good with cars, me. Now, back to business. What were you doing watching my house?'

'Can't answer that. Sorry.'

He breathed in then let it out with a long sigh. 'Mikey, our friend here needs a drink. Whyn't you get him one? The usual, I reckon.'

Mikey left the kitchen. In the moments he was gone I began to smell the heavy odour of maleness coming from Little Jimmy and the other goon, who refused to meet my eyes when I looked at him. Little Jimmy reached into my jacket and pulled out my wallet. He found one of my cards, which he read without expression and placed on the kitchen surface. 'Sparkle was right,' he said. 'Thought you'd turn up again. I'll take this card, if that's all right with you. Never know when I might need a private detective, Spud.'

The younger goon laughed, his coarse skin wrinkling like stiff paper being wrapped around a misshapen rock. Mikey and Spud. They were evidently going to be missed at the Bridge club tonight.

Mikey returned carrying an almost full bottle of vodka, which he opened and tipped to pour a couple of inches of clear liquid into a glass tumbler. Still saying nothing, and not having to be instructed, Spud stepped forward and gripped my jaw, forcing it open. Mikey then poured the drink down my throat while holding my nose. The liquid went down smoothly and then made its presence felt by stripping the back of my throat raw.

I gagged and spluttered. Jimmy patted me on the head. 'More where that comes from,' he said. 'Just be a good lad and spill the beans.'

There was a moment's pause as I caught my breath and Little Jimmy waited for me to tell him what I'd been doing. I turned my head slightly to look out into the garden. 'Nice shrubs,' I said.

'OK' Little Jimmy said, 'I had a feeling this was going to be hard. Let's go.' He stepped back, and Mikey and Spud grabbed me again and walked me out of the kitchen. We followed Jimmy across the foyer and through another door. This led down a flight of steps and opened into a larger room, now underground, which flickered as Jimmy switched on a fluorescent.

'Home sweet home,' he said.

The room was low-ceilinged and square, lacking windows and any other door. I felt my heart beat a little faster as Jimmy closed the door behind us. He nodded to Mikey again and they poured more vodka down my throat. I felt it going to my head this time as its fire touched my tongue and spread its warmth throughout my upper body.

In the centre of the room was a black leather chair mounted on a white hydraulic plinth, putting me in mind of a dentist's chair. Except there were black leather straps on the arms. I looked around the room. There was a work-top and a sink, a vice screwed to another stretch of worktop on the facing wall, a rack of tools containing hammers, files, screwdrivers, pliers, and then a separate rack that I realised was actually a display case. The men placed me in the chair and began to do up the straps across my wrists and around my legs. The chair moved slightly as I squirmed in it.

Looking across the room, I realised that the display case was lit from inside and was actually quite delicately made, as though it might contain the finer examples of a butterfly collector's art.

In fact it contained a selection of human fingers. Stumpy, delicate, pale, dirt-encrusted — the whole range of digits that a collector like Little Jimmy might amass through a life of diligence and care.

'Ah, you've seen them,' he said.

I turned back to him to see that from somewhere he'd picked up a pair of garden secateurs, and was casually opening and closing them. As if by their own will, my hands clenched into fists and tried to turn upwards into my jacket sleeves.

I looked up at him. 'What have you done with Kelly?' I asked.

He stopped flexing the secateurs and frowned at me. 'Who?'

'She was last seen here with you at a party. She hasn't been seen since that night.'

'So what? You think I've done something to her?'

He looked around at Mikey and the other man, inviting them to laugh with him. But they remained stony-faced.

'Why would I do that?' he said. 'With everything I've got going for me, why would I do something to a girl?'

'Because you're a sick bastard?' I said.

The smile on his face froze and he came closer. I could see the musculature under his tee-shirt and smell the testosterone seeping from him. He brought his face close to mine – so close I could see the pale stubble on his cheeks and the blood vessels in the corner of his eyes.

'Give him another drink, boys,' he said, without looking at them. At the same time, I felt him gripping my right hand

and beginning to uncurl my fingers. His own fingers were broad and stumpy—a builder's fingers, perhaps, used to throwing bricks around and wielding a mallet. Crude fingers, useful for bullying and pointing. Perhaps that was the attraction for him of other people's digits—in some way he was jealous of their hands, their delicacy.

My jaw was forced open again and more stinging vodka was poured down. Mikey held my nose till I spluttered and swallowed the drink.

Jimmy said, 'All right, boys, you can go back upstairs now. I won't need you for a while.'

'You'll be all right, Jim?' Mikey asked, looking from him to me as though I might break the straps, spring from the chair and lunge with both hands around Jimmy's neck.

'That's fine,' Little Jimmy said. 'I can handle this. Go upstairs and have a drink.'

Mikey hesitated for a moment then turned and followed his colleague, who had already lumbered from the room. The door shut behind him. It seemed very quiet all of a sudden.

'What do you think of the chair?' Jimmy asked, stepping back and letting go of my fingers. 'E-bay's a wonderful thing, sure. Where else would you go for a second hand dentist's chair? Cost me two grand, plus delivery. Had to put in the straps, of course, so there was a bit of work there. But worth the effort.'

'You're a sadist. What have you done with Kelly?'

'That girl again. I've told you, I know nuttin' about her. There might've been a party and I might've met her, but that's the last of it.' His eyes were pale blue and held no kind of feeling.

'You're lying.'

He had been circling me. Now he stopped and came close

again. Without warning he raised his fist and punched me in the face. I managed to turn away at the last minute so he caught my cheek bone instead of my nose. I closed my eyes and shook my head. When I opened them again, he was staring at me. He took another step forward, grabbing my right hand and splaying the fingers. After a second I felt the cool metal of the curved secateurs' blades run the length of each finger.

'Which one can you do without?' he said. 'I'll leave you the thumb, because I'm not that cruel. So—first finger? No more picking your nose or dialling old fashioned phones. Middle finger? You won't be able to give anyone the finger—because you won't have one. Third or fourth? Not much use for anything but counting with. So maybe we'll go for the ... Third.' He seized my hand tighter and started to isolate my third finger.

'You bastard.'

I was squirming hard now, trying to flex my hand away from his, but his grip was monstrous. His back was to me as he leaned over and with his left arm immobilised my right hand while he lined up the cutting blades. We struggled for some seconds.

'So what's this girl to you?' he asked, without looking at me.

'Let go and I might tell you,' I gasped.

'Cocky, aren't we,' he said, and stretched my fingers out. I felt the blades either side of my finger as they began to pinch. The skin on the finger began to tear and I wondered what it would be like to grip things without that finger to hold ...

Then the basement door opened and another figure appeared. He wore a white tee-shirt and his ginger hair was also cropped short. He looked like a normal version of Little

Jimmy, without the pumped-up muscles.
	Pete Wilder, Jimmy's older brother.

CHAPTER NINE

'Jimmy!' he said. 'What the fuck're you doing?'

Little Jimmy let go of my arm and stepped away. He stood facing his brother, breathing hard.

Pete said, 'What you up to, you daft fucker?'

Jimmy seemed to come out of a trance. He looked back at me, then at Pete, and shrugged. Pete nodded towards me and after a pause, Jimmy turned and undid the straps around my arms and legs.

'I don't like visitors,' he said quietly, looking up at me.

Pete was still in the doorway. A woman's face appeared behind him, thin and lined and smoking a cigarette. She wore a pink one-piece jump suit that made her look like a stick of marshmallow. Pete became aware of her. 'Marie—I told you to wait upstairs. Now go back.'

'I will not,' she said, her accent more Irish than Liverpudlian, and made hoarse by a lifetime of smoking. Pete came into the room suddenly, as if pushed in by Marie's willpower. Little Jimmy had finished untying my legs and I stood up from the chair.

'Do I know you?' Pete said.

'We've never met,' I said, rubbing my wrists. 'But I know about you and your brain-dead brother.'

Marie snorted a laugh and looked up at me. 'You've got balls, Mister.'

'Don't you talk like that about him,' Pete said. 'Or I'll have him strap you in the chair again.'

'Let him try when he hasn't got the Orcs to help him,' I said, and moved towards the door. The floor tipped up towards me and I reached out a hand, which Marie caught and held while I got my balance. I looked at her face and saw in that brief glimpse a weight of misplaced affection and grief and loneliness that cigarettes and probably booze were working hard to keep in check.

'Get away from these people, Marie,' I said quietly.

Her eyes registered what I'd said but she turned away so that she didn't have to reply.

'So mister,' Little Jimmy said to me before I left the room. 'Watch your step. Don't let me catch you round here again.'

I said nothing and stumbled up the stairs to the ground floor. Mikey was standing there with a bottle of Evian water in his hand. He caught me as I tripped again and led me towards the front door. The hallway moved in circles around me as I walked. He opened the door and took us out. Then he guided me over the gravel, past the red Corvette, and opened the large black gates. He gave me the bottled water from one hand and two Nurofen tablets from the other.

'Take these and drink the water before you go,' he said. 'You might make it back in one piece.'

'Thanks,' I said. 'Don't let him take you all down.'

'Fuck off and don't come back,' Mikey said, and shut the gates behind me. I walked back to the Cavalier and sank into the driver's seat. I drank the bottle and ate the tablets and an hour later felt sober enough to drive, though I probably wasn't.

By the time I got to Laura's house, she had already eaten and was working on her laptop on the table she called her office. She looked up when I came in and stopped what she was doing.

'You look terrible,' she said. She looked a little harder. 'Have you been drinking?'

'Not on purpose,' I said, and collapsed on to her sofa. The light was hurting my eyes so I closed them. When I opened them I seemed to be in bed and feeling more comfortable than I ever remembered feeling. Laura was leaning over me and saying something about drinking and driving, but her voice was tender and I didn't feel that I was being told off. Not much, anyway.

Later, she was in bed with me, her body pliant and warm against my side. It was dark outside but whether it was nine o'clock or the middle of the night, I had no idea.

'This job I've got,' I said.

'Yes?'

'The client is Dan.'

Her bedside light came on and I felt her raising herself on to one elbow to look down at me.

'Dan, your son? Who you've never met?'

'Until yesterday.'

'When were you planning to tell me?'

'I had no plans. It was just something that happened.'

There seemed to be a long silence. I might have fallen asleep again.

She said, 'Why didn't you tell me yesterday?'

'I was still trying to understand it—what it meant. I didn't know how you'd take it. I didn't want to have to deal with you as well as him.'

'Didn't it cross your mind that I might help?'

I couldn't answer that. She always outfoxed me.

'Didn't think of that, did you, tough guy? Still don't trust me, do you?'

'That's not true.'

'But if I can't help you, it's because you don't let me. You won't let me in, Sam. How much do you really trust me?'

'I'd trust you with anything.'

'Then why do you lie to me?'

'It wasn't a lie. I just didn't tell you everything.'

'Yes, there's a huge difference.'

At that point she turned over, put out the light, and as far as I could tell, went to sleep.

The next morning she was gone before I was awake.

CHAPTER TEN

The space was big enough for anyone—four paces across, each way. There was a bed, chest of drawers, a Sony mini sound system and he'd even given her an ipod, already loaded with his collection of 60s music. There was a shower cubicle and a toilet next to it, with a mirrored cabinet so she could do herself up if she felt like it. There was a fridge and a cooking hob next to each other, and beside them a sink with running water. Once she'd broken off the end of a Coke bottle and come at him, but she hadn't punctured the skin. He was a bit more careful now and made sure she was on the other side of the room when he went in.

He'd told the tradesmen he'd used that it was a Panic Room. But he'd always known it would be his cage. The place where he'd keep his trophies, until they came round. Until they were safe enough to be let out, to walk out with him in public.

The room was beginning to smell. She was an untidy bitch. He was always having to take her clothes away and burn them because she refused to use the washing machine. She didn't cook, either. Just used the microwave to heat up the ready meals he brought. He'd put in air vents but maybe he should have fitted an extractor to take away the smell. He knew that she never showered—maybe she was afraid he'd be watching in some way, through a peephole in the shower wall or something. Admittedly it had occurred to him, but he decided to give her that privacy at least. She deserved that.

Most of the time she was quiet, dreamy or sullen, staring away from him. She looked terrible. Not how she looked when he first saw her that night—energetic, her skin pink with excitement, her eyes glinting like knives. He'd wanted her straight away, and he'd had her, too.

He let down the last section of the folding ladder and dropped into the room. He placed the fresh linen he'd brought on the single chair and ripped off the dirty blankets from the bed. He'd burn them later, along with her dirty underwear, so that no one would see him doing women's laundry. He could burn what he liked on the site and no one would know anything.

She watched him from the corner of the room. Her blonde hair was straight and looked like it hadn't been washed in a week. She was biting her nails and spitting out pieces of dead skin.

'Do you want anything?' he asked.

'Yeah—lemme out.'

Little Jimmy laughed and shook his head. They had this routine now, which was good. It meant she was getting used to him. Not as frightened of him as she used to be.

'You've got to get clean first,' he said. 'You know the rules.'

'How am I gonna do that if you keep giving me junk?' she said fiercely.

'Do you want to go cold turkey? I can always arrange

that.'

'"Cold turkey",' she mocked. 'God, you're so stuck in the 60s, aren't you? Are you sure you're only thirty-five?'

She saw the look in his eyes and backed down, shifting her weight. He'd lied to her about his age, but he didn't like her questioning him.

'No, I don't wanna go cold turkey,' she said. 'It's the only thing I've got in here.'

Little Jimmy looked in the fridge and checked her supplies. 'I'll get you some more of those pasta meals,' he said. 'You like those, don't you?'

'I guess. Will you tell me something?'

'What's that, Princess?'

'Don't call me that. Is ... Is anyone looking for me?'

Little Jimmy stood upright. 'Why? Do you think anyone's going to miss you, a little whore?'

Her eyes became tearful. 'Don't laugh at me,' she said. 'Don't do that, it's not nice.'

He looked away from her. 'No—nobody's looking for you. You're a big blank space. What did you think—the cavalry's going to come over the hill, like, and take you away? Listen, get used to the idea of staying here for a while. When you're settled in we'll get you off the junk properly and take it from there.'

He heard the sound of his own voice and felt himself turning cold. He didn't like lying to her but she'd given him little choice. Always pushing at him, trying to get information or get him to do something for her. And he knew he was confused. He didn't have a plan. He liked the idea of her being with him, like a proper girlfriend. But he also knew that would never happen. He couldn't let her out, now she'd been here all this time. The man in the film had it wrong—they'd never get to know him properly. The real him. The one inside.

Now she moved away from the wall and came towards him. She was only wearing panties and a thin top, as she usually did, and he held his breath as she came close. Her body was slim and well-formed and seemed flawless, and it had always fascinated him.

'Jimmy,' she said, breathing softly. 'Did you bring me some fresh clothes?'

He pointed to the pile on the bed. She turned and riffled through the blankets until she came to the clean tee-shirts and underwear. Then she slowly slipped her panties off and turned to face him. She dropped them to the floor, crossed her arms and lifted off her cotton top. She smiled at him, then turned back to the bed and picked up a pair of fresh blue panties, which she stepped into. She held her hands in front of her breasts and spoke to him again.

'You don't visit me, Jimmy. Are you bored? Don't you like me any more?'

Jimmy's throat was dry and he swallowed to moisten it. He realised he'd been staring at her as though she'd hypnotised him. At the same time, he was embarrassed for her, using herself like this. He looked away from her breasts and found his voice.

'Pack it in,' he said, and began picking her old clothes from the floor. 'We've been through this before. You tell me what you want and I'll get it. You don't have to do this. It won't change anything.'

Her demeanour shifted again. She did that a lot, like a cat suddenly deciding to turn and spit at you for no good reason. It was as though she suddenly became sharp at the edges. Her lips grew thin and her eyes shrank to small slits. 'Bastard,' she said quietly. 'Let me go, you bastard! What are you trying to do to me? Whyn't you let me go, you son of a bitch!'

'I've told you before,' he said. 'Just a few more weeks—'

'Noooo!' she yelled, as though trying to make herself heard outside the brick prison in which she'd already spent the best part of a month. She ran to the sink, picked up a coffee mug and threw it at him. He let it bounce off his chest. It shattered on the tile floor. She threw an empty plastic milk bottle, a frozen lasagne in its packet and a box of tea bags. Jimmy ignored them. Kelly was now in full despair, crying and wailing and grasping for anything in reach. Jimmy watched her without emotion. He'd found that he could do that quite easily because he couldn't understand what drove people to those levels of anger. He was always calm.

Finally she threw herself on the bed and sobbed into the eiderdown. With one hand, Jimmy reached into his jeans pocket and found the wrap. He threw it on the bed next to her. A sixth sense told her to look up and she saw it immediately.

'I could take it away with me, if you like,' he said.

'Bastard bastard bastard.'

He reached down and picked up the packet. Her hand caught his before it had moved six inches. He saw her eyes, then, still greedy for the respite that the drug offered.

'Suit yourself,' he said, and dropped the packet again. He climbed back up the ladder, pulling it after him as he left the room.

He really didn't know what her problem was. He looked after her nicely, gave her food and clean clothes and just enough junk to keep her happy. It was her own stupid fault in the first place—she was in the wrong place at the wrong time. She shouldn't have been listening to him and Pete talk to that arsehole, Addison. She should just have walked away, instead of standing there with one hand on her hip, looking as though she had every right to listen in to people's private conversations.

He did want her to clean up, though. If he could get it through her head that he wouldn't have anything to do with her unless she was clean, then he'd consider letting her go. Okay he was feeding her habit, he knew that. But he was gradually reducing the amount he gave her. She didn't seem to have noticed yet, so perhaps his plan was working.

But he wasn't feeling as good as he wanted to. That guy from the other day—Dyke—had unsettled him. Why was he looking for Kelly? What the fuck did he have to do with her? Who'd sent him?

He didn't know whether he should tell Pete or not. He hadn't mentioned it—Pete had other things on his mind, which was why he'd called in unexpectedly that day and found him with Dyke. Jimmy told him that they caught the guy sitting outside looking at the house. He didn't mention Kelly and he didn't mention the fact that Dyke was a private investigator. Pete would go spare if he thought someone was looking for the girl. So it was best not to bring it up. Maybe he'd go after this Dyke character himself. After all, he had his business card, so he could easily find out where he lived.

Before that, though, he had another little plan. He was proud of this one because it made him feel good about something. He knew that Kelly had been turned on to junk by her first pimp, but since she'd come to Manchester she must have had a regular supply. So Jimmy was going to start a little war going. He and Pete were moving into Manchester anyway, so this was just adding spice to the mix.

He didn't mind gear and pills, and he didn't particularly mind cocaine. He was happy to regulate them and take a cut. Be crazy not to in this market. But junk was something different. It always had been, for him. People who put that stuff in their arms became useless as customers. They were more trouble than they were worth in the end. Besides, he'd seen it happen to his cousin Billy when he was young. He'd been a good laugh, Billy, but then he just drifted away. Became hollow. And then he died from a bad needle. Now Jimmy wouldn't touch junk as a business product. He had ethics where that was concerned.

So he might not be able to do anything about Dyke just yet, but heroin dealers, yeah, he could do something about them.

CHAPTER ELEVEN

The Nurofen had prevented a full-on hangover from taking hold, but I was still muzzy-headed when I woke the next morning. I made myself eat bacon and eggs and did some light gym-work before driving into my office. The roads were slick with overnight rain and a pall of grey hung over the town centre, as if the clouds were just waiting for another excuse to give us a good soaking.

One bill and one thank-you letter from a satisfied client constituted my entire post. I put the bill to one side and filed the thank-you letter in my testimonials folder, which wasn't as full as I would have liked. Most people didn't like using private investigators and cut short their relationship with me as soon as they could. After sending their payment cheque, they would rather forget I existed than go on a limb to write me a recommendation. In any service industry you're more likely to get complaints than thanks, so why should mine be any different?

After a cup of coffee, I rang Dickie Baines again. I could almost hear him shaking his head as I told him about my meeting with Little Jimmy Wilder.

'God's sake, Sam, I told you to go careful. That man's a nutter. He's got no sense of self-control.'

'Never mind that, Dickie. I need information. What can you tell me?'

'I've already told you more than I should. You know I'm not supposed to talk to you at all.'

I knew that. After I'd been eased out of Customs and Excise I'd been blacklisted, though no one said as much. Only Dickie's complete disregard of bureaucracy gave me any contact at all with the people that I'd spent a good part of my working life with.

'Point me in the right direction, Dickie. You must know someone.'

I knew Dickie was well-connected. It was partly why he was such a good investigator.

'There's a guy in Liverpool,' he said eventually. 'Trevor Clarke. Works on a local rag. He's been following the twins for years. I'll give you his number and you can go and bother him for a while.'

He read out the number and after we'd talked a little more, I hung up and rang Trevor Clarke. A bored receptionist put me through to his desk and he answered immediately. I told him who I was and why I was calling.

'The twins?' he said. 'You mean someone's finally taking them bastards seriously? That's worth a pint. Come on over and we'll have a chat.'

I drove along the M56 and through Runcorn, over the vast steel bridge, then past the fan-shaped modern-art sculptures either side of the road that were probably some kind of symbol of regeneration. John Lennon airport sat behind the houses somewhere on my left, hidden by the commonplace suburbia that Lennon had railed against all his life.

Aigburth ran parallel to the Mersey and the place still had the vitality and diversity that characterised it in the nineteenth century. I found the café that Clarke had mentioned and parked in a side street.

Clarke probably wasn't much older than me, but I was happy to think he looked more weathered. He stood and introduced himself and his teeth were brown with nicotine stains; his jacket also smelled of nicotine. It looked fairly new but I had a hunch that if he'd been able to get hold of a tweed jacket with leather elbow-patches, he would have put in a smart bid for it.

'Sit thee down, sit thee down,' he said. 'Can I get you something?'

I asked for a coffee and he went to the counter and fetched one. It came with a small Italian biscuit in a cellophane wrapper.

Clarke began to tell me about the Wilder twins. Brought up by a strong mother who'd died fifteen years ago, there was a long pattern of anti-social behaviour running through their veins. Now in their late thirties, they both had juvenile records but then cleaned up their act—at least on the surface. Their cleverness resided in keeping their operation low-key. By attracting minimum attention to themselves, they'd been able to maintain the front of respectable builders towards those people who didn't know them or their history.

'Unbelievable,' I said.

'Not really,' Clarke said. 'Fill in the paperwork properly and run your business according to strict accountancy regulations and there's no reason for people to suspect that you're actually robbing bastards.'

'So at the moment they're builders.'

'Last fifteen years or so. Started with small plots, a few

private houses. Then they got into council estates, sub-contracting cardboard boxes. Now they're buying land cheap and putting up executive four-bed mock-Tudor monstrosities that will collapse in ten years, unless the paint happens to keep them upright.'

'You're no friend of theirs.'

'I've known some people live in their houses. You wouldn't put a dog in them, unless you happened to hate the dog.'

'Don't people complain?'

'Let's say they don't get very far. The regulations are adhered to – as a humble consumer, what more can you do?'

'So what are they up to at the moment?'

'Tendering for bigger projects with the council.' He pulled his chair closer to the table and looked me in the eye. 'I understand this is a cut-throat business. Builders have to do the best they can and still make money. I understand that. But there've been rumours about the Ginger Twins for years.'

'What kind of rumours?'

'You can guess. They've got permission to build where others haven't. They always manage to undercut the competition. None of it makes the bigger papers, despite my best efforts, and none of it deflects them off course. They're always there, putting in that tender, treated with respect by the council or the trust or whoever it happens to be that holds the money.'

'You're sure you're not just a suspicious old bastard?'

Clarke laughed. 'Oh, I'm that all right. Listen, there's a big permission going through at the moment for some houses to be built near a new supermarket on the Dorset Estate. There's a strip of land that's been under debate for years, but no one's ever got permission to build on it before now.'

'Why not?'

'Take your pick. Ecology. Some Nimbies, some local objections. People say new houses will devalue their own properties. It was bad enough when the supermarket went up—they had to promise to put in traffic lights and a new roundabout and everything. This new housing, though, is getting the locals tearing their hair out. Some of them are going to lie down in front of the bulldozers when they come in.'

'And are the Wilders going to get the permission to build?'

'That's the way it's looking at the moment. They've even had people there measuring up with theodolites and so forth, as if the job's already been decided.'

Clarke was animated—fired up by the apparent injustice of the Wilders getting their way without any opposition.

'What's in it for you?' I asked. 'Why are you so het up?'

'I just want to see those bastards get what's coming to them. They've had their way too long in this town and I suppose they deserve a comeuppance.'

'And where's the objective journalist?'

'Waiting to see them get a good kicking.'

I left Clarke rolling a cigarette and waiting for another cup of black coffee to be delivered. I wasn't sure that I trusted his motives and that his information was 100 per cent accurate, but his passion was infectious. He seemed eager for me to get involved, but that was all right. I was eager to get involved too.

From a phone box directory I found the number of the local council and rang the Planning Office. Eventually I was put through to a man called Addison, who was abrupt, not too friendly, and clearly didn't want to talk to me.

When I told him I wanted to discuss the Dorset Estate, the line went even cooler.

'Who did you say you were?' he asked.

I repeated the lie that had got me this far. 'Joe Gorman. I've just joined the local residents' group and I wanted to ask how things are standing with the permission.'

'I'm afraid I can't talk about that. We'll make our decision shortly and it will be published in the usual way. The minutes of all the meetings will appear on our website.'

'Can you give us a clue which way the decision might go?'

'Mr Gorman, you have to understand that you can't talk to a council official like this. We have to be completely unbiased and make our decisions unswayed by any information other than that which comes to us through formal channels. If you have anything to say, I suggest you go that route.'

'If you don't mind me saying, Mr Addison, you sound like a bit of a pompous prat. Will you take that into account when making your decision?'

I hung up before he found the words to say anything.

CHAPTER TWELVE

Trevor Clarke had given me the address of the Twins' offices. I drove north along Derby Road, parallel to the Mersey, and found their building, part of a large complex five minutes' walk from the river. Where once the docks were packed with large redbrick warehouses, now they're mostly single-story modern fabrications surrounded by large car parks. I wondered why the Twins had taken offices here if they weren't involved in shipping. A sign outside read 'Wilder Shores Ltd,' which was more poetic than I thought they were capable of. A bored girl sat behind a counter playing solitaire on her computer and guarding a telephone on which a single red light blinked constantly. She turned her wide eyes on me and asked if she could help.

'Are Peter or James expected today?'

'Who? ... Oh you mean Little Jimmy.' She suddenly remembered her job and straightened up. 'I'm sorry, sir, they're not in at the moment. They're on site, but I am expecting them later. Can I make an appointment for you?'

'Don't bother. Tell them Sam was here. They'll know who

it was.'

She took a pad and laboriously wrote down my name using all her powers of concentration. I looked around the office but there was nothing to see: a photocopier, fax machine, wire mail basket. A door behind the receptionist went further into a warehouse but its glass window was blocked off by a calendar showing two girls without their tops cuddling up to each other.

'Anything else, sir?' the girl asked.

'Yes—if I were you I'd look for another job. Not many prospects here.'

I left before she managed to formulate a response. I was getting good at that.

I went back to my car and waited. I didn't know what I expected to see, but the art of superior private detection is rather like being a good football striker—being in the right place at the right time. It was the middle of the afternoon so I thought I'd give it a couple of hours and see who turned up.

Twenty-one minutes later, Little Jimmy's red Corvette turned the corner and parked in a marked bay opposite his office. Another van with blacked-out windows pulled up behind it and Mikey and Spud got out. They stood around while Little Jimmy finished a phone call before pulling himself out of the low-slung car.

Then, as I watched, a series of extraordinary events unfolded.

First, Dan and Pedlar John emerged from a gap between two buildings and approached Little Jimmy. One of them must have said something because the heads of all three gangsters turned towards them. Mikey and Spud detached themselves from their positions leaning on the bonnet of their van and moved to intercept Dan, but Little Jimmy put out a hand and said something and they stopped as if invisible reins had pulled them short.

I had my hand on the door handle, ready to move, but Little Jimmy just stood and watched as Dan approached with his finger pointed at Jimmy's chest and speaking fast. I noticed that Pedlar John had slowed his pace and was well back, eyeing Mikey nervously.

Little Jimmy said something. Then Dan said something. They went back and forth for a minute or so, then Little Jimmy must have made a sign or said something else, because Mikey and Spud suddenly stepped forward and grabbed Dan by the arms. At this point, Pedlar John made a run for it and they let him go. Little Jimmy said something more to his valiant men, then turned and walked towards his office. Mikey and friend marched Dan to their van, put him between them on the front bench seat, and drove off.

I turned the ignition and followed.

We drove away from the river, out of the dock area and along Millers Bridge, then up Breeze Hill heading towards Walton. Eventually we hit the residential district of suburban homes, leisure clubs and tennis courts. After ten minutes, the van turned off a main road and after a couple of further turns slowed and crunched onto the mixed earth and gravel base of a building site. The site was boarded up from the main road, with a gap in the boards allowing the only access on to the site. Colourful signs nailed to the boards warned against venturing inside and listed various regulations with which the contractors were compliant.

I parked opposite and ran across the street. The site was deserted, with no sign of work having been done for some time. A shell of a large family house was half-completed, the drains visible in deep-cut trenches, the walls of the house still missing windows, doors and roof. A small yellow digger stood to one side, a dirty tarpaulin draped over its cab. Further into the site, the van which I'd been following was parked outside a grey Portakabin plastered with Health and Safety notices and raised up on bricks. I ran across the muddy ground, and as I got to the door I heard a series of thumps and thuds from inside. I took the steps in one leap and crashed through the door.

What I saw didn't square with what I expected to see. Spud was on all fours, clutching a bloody nose. He was making moaning sounds from the back of his throat. Beside him, facing off against each other were Mikey and Dan, who seemed to be in some kind of pose, his hands held open-palmed before his chest and one leg raised in front of the other. Mikey looked surprised by any number of factors — his colleague on the ground, Dan's aura of confidence, me standing in the doorway like a rabid dog. And just as Mikey registered that it was me, Dan took off in a spin the like of which I'd only seen Bruce Lee achieve and caught him flush on the jaw with a roundhouse kick. Mikey collapsed like someone had cut his strings and fell in an untidy heap.

'Hi, Dad,' Dan said, still bouncing on his feet. He looked down at Mikey, then at me, and let the tension out of his body. 'Tae Kwon Do,' he said. 'You weren't worried, were you?'

CHAPTER THIRTEEN

The discussion in my car was going well.

'Well you're not doing anything, are you?' Dan said. 'I've seen more commitment from a fly trying to climb out a window. Good job I'm not paying you.'

'You don't know what you're talking about.'

'So have you found anything yet? Are you any closer to finding Kelly?'

I didn't want to tell him about my meeting with Little Jimmy or what Sophie had told me about Kelly meeting the Wilders at the party. He didn't need to know more about how badly Kelly was treating him.

'What did you say to him?' I asked.

'Who?'

'Jimmy Wilder. Outside his office. Where you could have got your brains kicked in.'

Dan shrugged. 'I asked him what he'd done with Kelly.'

'And that went down well?'

'What do the papers say?—he denied all knowledge of her. Lying arsehole.'

'Then what happened?'

'I told him I was going to be watching him.'

'You threatened a gangster,' I said. 'Cool move.'

'You saw his crew. Couple of prats.'

I couldn't argue with that. I said, 'You should phone me. Let me know what you're doing.'

He mumbled something, his head turned towards the window.

'What?'

'I've lost my phone. I haven't had one for a week.'

I started to shake my head—but then something occurred to me.

'Why did Pedlar John take us to that bookshop in Manchester?' I asked.

'You turn on a sixpence, don't you?'

'I want to know why Pedlar John chose that bookshop, which happens to be owned by the Wilders.'

Dan looked ahead for a moment. 'He said that Sparkle was someone he'd had dealings with, and was someone who knew ... Girls like that. Why? What does it matter?'

'I don't understand why John took us there first. If we were supposed to be just asking questions, how come we started there?'

'As good a place as any—someone who knows the girls on the streets.'

'And has a direct line to the Wilders.'

'What's that supposed to mean?'

'I don't like your so-called friend. I don't understand why he's caught up in this. I don't understand why he's helping you out. He strikes me as the kind of person who only does things that are going to contribute to his own pension plan.'

Dan snorted and turned away.

'You see what you want to see,' he said.

'Well do you think he's helped so far? This bull in a china shop routine? I'm going to lay down some rules. I do this for a living. I know what I'm doing and I know what works. He's an amateur, a busybody and someone who's looking out for himself. I wouldn't trust him to clean my shoes.'

'You don't have to trust him. That's my department. He's the one who got me up here. He's the one who's given me a bed to sleep on. He's the one who tells me what's he's up to. You're the one I think I ought to sack, not him.'

Another silence. We were almost home now, the journey having gone past like a film on fast-forward.

'You and Pedlar John are keeping something from me,' I said. 'I don't know what you're up to, but there's something you haven't told me, isn't there?'

Dan took a packet of mint tictacs from his pocket and dropped one into his hand, then flipped it into his mouth. He chewed for a couple of minutes before turning to look at me sideways.

'We thought if you knew, you wouldn't help,' he said.

'Knew what?'

'You asked whether Kelly did drugs.'

He weighed up whether he had to say any more but I pre-empted him.

'I get it,' I said.

'Don't judge her. She's had it tough at home, and she's been trying to get off them. You don't have any right to judge her.'

I bit my lip. He was right. If I'd known she was hooked, I would have kicked him out of the office, son of mine or no.

'She was doing really well,' he said.

'Why did she leave?'

He glanced at me. 'Yeah, all right, we had a row. I caught her shop-lifting when we were out. She said she had no money and didn't know how else to get it.'

'Do her parents know what's going on with her?'

'Sore point. She had a rough time with her dad, but she wouldn't tell me anything about him. Not around much, very strict, mother a wet blanket. I'm sure you've heard all this before in your tough life.'

'You look at anyone long enough you can convince yourself they've had a bad time.'

He ignored me.

'It's not as if they didn't try to help her,' he said. 'She didn't get on with her dad. They even came over here to get her away, to like broaden her horizons.'

'Came over here from where?'

'The States. She's American. Didn't I say?'

I thought of the American voice who'd answered the phone when I rang the number Sophie had given me. The trouble was, I didn't know whether that cleared up a mystery or created another one.

Before we arrived at Dan's place, I stopped at a supermarket and bought him a pay-as-you-go mobile phone. He hung around until I'd got through the till, then took the box from me and started unwrapping it. I made sure I took a note of the number and put it on a card, which I dropped in my pocket. He mumbled a thank-you then wandered off, focused on identifying all the toys on the phone. I walked outside to get cash from the hole in the wall.

When I returned to the front entrance, he had exercised his prerogative and left.

CHAPTER FOURTEEN

I bought fish and chips and went home to eat. The car stank of vinegar by the time I parked and went inside. Laura had left a message on my answer phone saying that she was staying at her place tonight. I had expected it. Keeping my contact with Dan from her had not been a good move.

In fact I wasn't upset by her absence. Since I'd burst into the Portakabin and found Dan posing like a praying mantis, ready to drop kick Mikey into the next postcode, I'd been feeling pretty stupid. I was all wound up to come on like the protective dad, and he just didn't need it. He'd told me that the one good thing his foster parents had done for him was pay for Tae Kwon Do lessons when he was a teenager. He hadn't wanted to go initially but found that he was light on his feet and picked up the discipline quickly. He'd won a couple of competitions and then got bored.

But something else had been bothering me about the situation. We'd been on a building site in the middle of the afternoon, but there was no one about. The materials were covered with tarpaulins which were not only tied down, they were attached to spikes hammered into the ground, as if they were there for the long term. The whole place, including the Portakabin itself, had the air of being abandoned, as if no work had been carried out on site for weeks or even months.

I sat and ate my fish and chips at the kitchen table, staring at a newspaper but not reading. I was liking all this less and less, but I didn't know where to start. I didn't think I could stomach yet another drive to Liverpool.

But as the evening wore on I found I couldn't concentrate. I couldn't sit or listen to music or numb out in front of the television.

The clock in the Cavalier was reading 8.57 when I climbed inside and headed north.

The site was untouched since I'd been there. Mikey and his pal had gone, and they'd made an attempt to fix up the door by nailing a couple of planks across it, but nothing else had changed. The gate barring entrance into the site had long since had its lock smashed, but this was a polite suburban area and no further damage had been done to the materials inside. Maybe potential vandals knew who ran the site and steered clear.

I stood with my back to the Portakabin and looked around. House shell off to my right, oddly bleak in its half-finished state, as though it were located in Lebanon or Bosnia, not a back street of suburban Liverpool. To my left, half a dozen humped mounds like the carcasses of lumpy beasts. These were piles of bricks, timbers, bags of concrete and sand that had been covered with tarpaulins and abandoned. Further back was the dim outline of the digger, bowed like a prehistoric creature that hadn't yet evolved into a velociraptor or Tyrannosaurus Rex. Surrounding the whole area was a wall of giant compressed wood sheets like those used to board up the windows of empty houses. It was a tiny plot of savagery in the otherwise placid suburbs.

I walked over to the house and stepped through the frame of the doorway. The concrete base had been laid but none of the utilities was yet connected. There was no plumbing, no electricity cabling. The brick walls were still unplastered. In the corner of the largest room, presumably the lounge, were the remains of a wood fire. It seemed that squatters were now moving in before the house was even finished and occupied. Exercising a true entrepreneurial spirit and cutting out the middle man. I walked through the house to the back door and looked out into what would eventually become the garden, but at the moment was a muddy field churned by workmen's feet and crusted with bits of broken brick and metal. The dim moonlight and faint peripheral glow from nearby houses threw distorted shadows over the patch of rough ground. The back of the garden was bounded by new panel fencing, and in one corner, where a shed and a compost heap were destined to appear, another pile of materials crouched in darkness.

I stepped into the mud and walked across, then stopped. What I had thought was another consignment of timber covered by a tarpaulin was in fact a rolled up carpet.

I knelt down and tugged at one edge of the carpet and eventually released it. Then I moved down and unfurled the edge from the weight that was holding it together. As I pulled the final section, the whole thing unravelled and fell open.

And the decaying body of a young woman wearing only a delicate shift rolled over, threw out a weary arm and looked straight up at the stars.

My call to the police was brief but effective. Within fifteen minutes two cars rolled up and four young uniforms walked tentatively through the mud, into the house and, judging by the torchlight I saw from across the road, into the back garden. Moments later one of them ran back to his car and got on the radio. Within another twenty minutes a further two cars and a couple of vans turned up. I'd been crouching behind a hedge while all this detection had been going on, but I thought it was now probably a good time to leave.

As I walked away I called Trevor Clarke on the mobile number he'd given me. He didn't answer, but I left a message telling him to watch the local news.

The next night and the following day the case of the 'body in the carpet' made national as well as local media. I'd seen that it wasn't Kelly immediately – the girl had black hair and a long jaw, and the shape of her face was different to the girl in the photo Dan had shown me. But I was sad for her and her parents anyway, whoever they were.

Laura got over her huff and on Saturday night came to sit with me as we watched shaky footage of the Ginger Twins being hauled in for questioning. They cropped up on most of the TV news shows, their black and white tee-shirts and bulging muscles becoming familiar to news junkies up and down the country. Local reporters angling for prime-time coverage stood outside the courts and issued dramatic bulletins of the legal wrangling going on inside.

'What horrible-looking men,' Laura said, as yet more footage of the Twins walking into the station house spooled across the screen.

'Don't judge them on looks alone,' I said. 'Take into account their horrible personalities, too.'

'I can't watch,' she said. 'The thought of you having

anything to do with them is vile.'

She went into the kitchen to prepare dinner. She didn't stay that night, and when she left she gave me a kiss and a look that seemed to be half concern and half weariness with my continued insistence on putting myself in harm's way. Or maybe that was just my interpretation.

Before I went to bed, the phone rang.

'Is it Kelly?' Dan asked.

'No, it's not Kelly.'

'How can you be sure?'

I don't know why I hesitated but he sensed it. He said, 'You knew, didn't you? You found out.'

'It's not Kelly. The police will identify her soon.'

'Were you there?'

'Let's say I had a hunch.'

'And why didn't you tell me? How long were you going to let me stew, wondering whether it was her?'

He was right. I should have told him. But I hadn't wanted him to be any more involved than he had to be, so I kept quiet. Bad move.

'Anything else you haven't told me?' he asked.

'Not that I can think of. Go to bed.'

'Just don't lie to me any more. I've had enough of people lying to me.'

He hung up.

On Monday the Twins were released for lack of evidence. It seemed that the girl, still unnamed, had died of a drug overdose and had probably been dumped on the site. This time the Twins were filmed emerging triumphant from the police station, waving their joined hands aloft like victorious athletes. Their lawyers, silky men in brown suits, stood behind with their heads bowed, as if they didn't want to be recognised. I turned the television off in disgust.

That was when my trouble with the Twins really began.

CHAPTER FIFTEEN

Tuesday morning I toasted the last two slices of bread in the house. I sat and read the sports pages, then decided that this was too much excitement and I needed to go to work. I had bills to pay, and I couldn't find any more threads to pull on with Kelly. Besides, when you need creative thinking it's good to focus on something different.

Ken Bullard worked in a warehouse stacking pallets of machine tools. One day eight months ago, his mate Alfie had backed up the fork-lift six inches too far and hit a pile of empty pallets. They'd fallen on Ken's leg, necessitating thirty stitches down his right calf and a good deal of physiotherapy. His employers had been happy to pay his eight weeks statutory sickness pay, seeing as Ken was an employee in good standing of over ten years. But now they had called me in to find out whether Ken was doing the two-step around the official regulations, claiming benefit for which he was no longer eligible.

Ken lived in a small terrace in Coppenhall, a suburb of Crewe industrialised over a hundred years ago when cottages were built to house workers on the railways. At one time over twenty thousand people sweated and spilt blood to build the locomotives that had criss-crossed the country spewing out smoke. Now there might have been five hundred workers, toiling in the crumbling works that still stood in the gaps between the supermarket and the leisure park.

I tucked the Cavalier into a gap in the row of cars at the end of Ken's street and waited. I'd been watching him on and off for a couple of weeks. He had a routine that involved meeting his mates at the local pub at lunchtime, driving his wife to the shops on Wednesday morning, and helping his son-in-law renovate a canal boat at the marina in Nantwich at least two days a week. He limped by supporting his right leg with a stick and putting weight on the left. I hadn't seen him vary from this in the three weeks I'd been watching.

After fifty three minutes he came out of the house, climbed into his five-year-old Focus, and pulled away. I put the Cavalier into gear and followed. He made two left turns and was soon on his way out to the Marina, five miles distant, leaving the grimy edge of Crewe and crossing into the upmarket air of Nantwich, a cosy market town.

Eleven minutes later, according to the log that I kept, we arrived at the Marina. Once at the canal side, he parked and limped down the ranks of narrow boats until he came to the Empress of the Sea. He stepped carefully on board and knocked on the small door into the wheelhouse. After a moment his son-in-law, Clive, opened up and Ken went inside. Clive propped the door open despite the cool weather. The air inside was about to get powdery and choking. After a few minutes, I climbed out of my car, looked around innocently, and walked down the tow-path. As I came closer to the open door of the boat, I heard the high whine of a wood-cutting tool. Clive and Ken were cutting the long sheets of ply that would line the inside of the boat. I turned around and drove back to my office, clocking my miles for the sake of expenses. Whatever else he was, Ken was a good father-in-law. Helpful. It seemed that for some people, family was important. My dad had been important to me in ways that I hadn't realised until he'd died. Dan had lived with a stand-in father who he hadn't yet talked about. I began to wonder what impression he had of me – and what I could do to change it.

The rest of the day I spent wrestling with invoices and book-keeping, the curse of the self-employed. By five o'clock I'd had enough of paperwork, realising yet again that I'd left Customs Excise at least partly because of the bureaucracy. I drove home, ate by myself, talked briefly and inconclusively to Laura on the phone, and went to bed early. Fourth rule of private eye school: get as much sleep as you can. You never know when you might need it.

The next morning I thought I'd give Ken another chance to prove both me and the benefit office wrong. I left the house and lifted the door of the up-and-over garage, and was confronted with mayhem.

My battered Vauxhall Cavalier had been spattered and sprayed a sickly mustard-yellow. It looked as though several buckets of vomit had been dumped on it. The windscreen and both side windows were smashed and more paint had been tipped inside, covering the seats and the piles of cds that I left in the rear. All of this done without tripping my alarm or waking me. Serious professionals had done this and for a minute my blood ran cold.

I went back inside and checked all the rooms. Nothing was disturbed except my equilibrium. So the Ginger Twins weren't going to take a challenge to their freedom lying down. And they knew I was the one to blame for their latest difficulties. I guessed Mikey had recognised me just before Dan had knocked him out in the Portakabin. They must have put the story together afterwards that I'd found the girl's body and released the information to the police. It was a fair guess and I couldn't blame them for it. Sam Dyke, charitable detective.

I called Laura and checked that she was OK. She was busy and didn't have any time to spend commiserating with me. I had the distinct impression that she thought it was my own fault. She may well have been right. I rang Dan's new phone too but there was no reply, so I left a message.

Early afternoon I negotiated with a local body-shop I knew to do the repair work and they promised me a courtesy car, which turned out to be a two-year old navy-blue Astra. I signed the relevant papers then got in the car and drove to my office. The car was light compared to the Cavalier but had plenty of punch in the mid-range.

I went into my office warily but nothing had been touched. I checked my messages and switched on my computer. No phone calls, no emails. I sat in my chair and stared out of the window at the streets of Crewe town centre. People went about their business completely oblivious to the devastation that had taken place in my garage. How could they? Did they have no heart?

I tried Dan's mobile again and got voice mail again. I left another message for him to call me. I tried Laura but this time she was in a meeting and couldn't come to the phone.

I looked out of my window some more. For the sake of variety I tapped my fingers on my desk.

Admit it Dyke, I told myself, you're stumped.

My instinct was to get in the punchy Astra and drive

straight out to the Wirral to ask the Twins what the hell they thought they were doing. But on second thoughts I guessed this probably wasn't a good move. They wanted to rile me and punish me, so I couldn't let them think that they'd managed it. Far better to keep a dignified silence until a better opportunity came up.

I'd been fretting my way through a packet of Rolos and had almost finished them when my phone rang. The clock on my wall said it was 3:34 and I'd been in work exactly an hour. I snatched up the receiver and identified myself.

After a pause of about five seconds, a male voice with a Liverpool accent said, 'How do you like the new decor?'

Then hung up. I put down the handset and leaned back in my chair. Now what?

Then I drove home.

I walked through the front door and looked in the downstairs rooms. They'd done another comprehensive job. The kitchen was untouched, but the lounge was a scene of destruction: my cream sofa was slashed; facing it, the television was thrown face down so the glass was cracked; to its left, the curtains were torn from the windows; to its right, the CD player was ripped from its nest and the caddy broken. On the far wall, the Ikea CD shelving still stood but was bare, the cds having been pulled from the shelves and herded into a group on the floor. What really angered me was that they'd walked up and down over the cds, smashing the cases and most of the cds themselves. Two of the walls had also been unimaginatively spray-canned—'Cock' and 'Piss' being the limit of their literary aspiration. As I crouched and began to sort through the cds for undamaged cases, a migraine began its slow ascent from the back of my head to its usual squatting place over my right eye.

After tidying up the floor space, I picked up the phone and reported the break-in to the police. The weary uniform at the other end of the line asked me if anyone was hurt and then said they'd send someone round. I rang Laura on her work and mobile numbers but got no reply from either. I then rang Dan's number again but was put straight through to voice mail. Why is no one ever available when you really want them?

CHAPTER SIXTEEN

Upstairs there was more graffiti but no damage. It was as if they'd run out of steam by the time they'd climbed the stairs.

I worked on the house for a couple of hours, recompiling the cds, sweeping the carpets, putting the smashed television upright and fixing the audio equipment as best I could. Unusually, the work seemed to ease my headache; movement and concentration often exacerbates the thudding pain. A couple of policemen came and I told them what I'd found and when. They made some notes, then left. I took the torn curtains down and re-hung some old ones that I'd changed a few months ago, then tried to scrub off the flame-red graffiti. The writing wouldn't scrub, so I drove the two minute trip to the B Q by the train station and bought a five-litre can of one-coat emulsion and a fresh roller. I threw dust-covers over the furniture and began to paint.

It was getting dark outside when the front door opened and Laura came in with Dan.

'Jesus,' he said, staring round with an open mouth.

'Do you like what I've done with the place?' I said.

Laura stood in the doorway clutching her handbag, then made her way to the kitchen carrying an aura of cold fury with her.

'Have you got another brush?' Dan asked. I directed him to my shed and he came back a few minutes later having taken off his jacket and with his sleeves rolled up.

An hour later Laura came in carrying two plates of sausage and mash, which she handed to us silently. We sat on the edge of the ripped sofa and ate hungrily while Laura stood in the doorway and nibbled an apple like an ant attacking a watermelon.

'Are you going to say anything?' I asked.

'Nothing to say. You've got it all in hand, haven't you?'

I was quiet for a few minutes. 'The police say there's not much chance of catching who did it.'

'Did you give them a clue?'

'Not really. The Twins would have alibis. The people who got in would have been wearing gloves.'

'It's a message, right?' Dan said.

I nodded, putting down my plate. 'They want me to know that they know. They're saying butt out now before it gets worse.'

'But you're not going to, are you?'

I looked at Laura, but talked to Dan. 'Do you think Kelly's in danger?'

'How do I know? If she's with the Twins then I suppose she must be.'

Laura said, 'But you don't know whether she's with them because she wants to be. What if she likes it—all that stuff about women and power, you know.'

'From what I've heard, it's unlikely,' I said. 'They're creeps. Kelly must have seen that.' I looked from Laura to Dan and back again. Something that had been at the back of my mind suddenly came to the front. 'How come you two arrived together? You've never met. And where have you been? I've been trying to phone you.'

Dan turned sheepish and looked at Laura, who came into the room and sat. She said, 'When I was here on Saturday I found a piece of card on the kitchen floor. A phone number with Dan's name next to it.'

I remembered that I'd written down the number of his new mobile phone. I must have dropped it. I also remembered the odd look Laura had given me when she left—perhaps it was guilt, after all.

Laura went on. 'I phoned Dan and we met this lunchtime and talked. I told Dan about his mother, about you, about how you and I met.'

A man with a large ego and no sense of restraint had killed Dan's mother and her new husband, my client. Laura had worked for my client in his business, which is how we had met.

I looked at Dan. 'So what do you think?'

'What am I supposed to think? You might not have known about me until last Christmas, but you haven't been in touch since.'

'It wasn't that easy.'

'Oh, get over yourself,' he said, then stood up and took his plate into the kitchen. Laura was looking at me, shaking her head.

'Give him something,' she said. 'He doesn't know what he's doing. You've got to help him out.'

'I can't help him if I don't know what I'm doing.'

She stood up. 'Then tell him that. I know you're a man and you don't like to hear this, but you're not supposed to know all the answers.'

'Then what use am I?' I asked.

She left.

Dan stayed with me that night and helped finish the painting and tidying-up. Laura went back to her own house, pleading an early-morning meeting for which she needed a good night's sleep without the distractions of a broken house around her.

I gave Dan a glass of wine and we sat staring at the cracked television screen. I'd had it thirteen years so it was probably due for a change.

'Laura's got me a job,' he said suddenly.

'Always good to have an income.'

'They were looking for an office junior anyway—filing, taking phone calls, taking stuff to clients, that sort of thing. I start next week.'

'What about Pedlar John?'

'What about him?'

'Won't he get jealous? Think you've sold out to the Man?'

Dan took a sip from his glass. He looked tired and had swatches of Sunshine Yellow in his dark hair. 'I think you've got the wrong idea about me and him. He's just someone I know. He's barely even a friend. He had some information that was useful. I might live in his place, but we're not in each other's pockets.'

'Seen him around lately?'

'Not since he ran away from Little Jimmy's men the other day. He's probably embarrassed. He talks a good fight but his legs are made of jelly.'

'I would have said blancmange, but I'm not going to argue the toss.'

We grinned at each other.

The next morning I got up early and made breakfast: grilled

bacon, tomato, baked beans and toasted bagels. Dan walked in sleepily as I was laying out the table. He fetched himself fresh orange juice and sat at the table staring out of the patio window at the pale light from an April morning. The daffodils were still out but were beginning to sag.

'What we doing today?' he asked as I put his plate in front of him.

'We're doing nothing. I'm going to talk to Pete Wilder.'

'You've got a real death wish, haven't you?'

'You've got to front up to these guys. They respect you for it.'

I hoped I sounded more confident than I felt. I was only going to see Wilder because I couldn't think what else to do.

'I want to come,' Dan said around a mouthful of bagel.

I shook my head. 'No way. I don't want them seeing you again.'

'They already know me.'

'But they might not know you're connected to me. And they have my name and address, as we know.'

'I could help. Two of us is better than one.'

'I said no, Dan. This work isn't safe. I can't put you in danger.'

He stopped eating. 'You know I'll just come anyway. Two trains and a cab and I'll be on the doorstep with you.'

'You'd be putting Kelly in more danger.'

'You don't know that. What if you need someone to make a distraction while you go in the back way?'

I stood and took my plate to the kitchen. 'What do you think this is?' I said. 'Mission Impossible? I won't need a distraction or a kung-fu-kicking partner. I'm just going to talk to the man.'

'Then I'll sit in the car. If that's all it is, then I can't do any harm, can I?'

I rinsed my plate under the tap and put it on the drainer. My head was beginning to buzz. When I went back into the lounge he was still at the table but had finished his breakfast. He had woken up now and watched me keenly.

'You stay in the car,' I said.

'Okay.'

'You don't get out for any reason.'

'Okay.'

'If there's an earthquake you get in the back seat and put your fingers in your ears. You do not get out of the car.'

'I get the picture.'

'I don't think you do. But there's nothing I can do to make you see it, is there?'

'You can't scare me while you're wearing that apron.'

I went back into the kitchen and took off the apron. Then we drove north.

CHAPTER SEVENTEEN

Pete Wilder's house was two streets away from his brother's. It was a corner plot with high hedges and well-kept, tall poplars forming the edges of his territory. Many of the houses were secluded, behind hedges, at the end of long drives. It was hard to know exactly what kind of community this was, and what kind of people lived here. Probably businessmen from Liverpool or Manchester with fat pensions and no idea who Karl Marx was—unless he was one of those comedy brothers in old films.

I drove past the house and parked out of sight, then we sat and waited for half an hour.

'What are we doing?' Dan asked. 'We can't see the house so are we using telepathy, or what?'

'Patience, dear boy.'

'How will we be able to tell if anyone's in unless we knock on the door?'

'Breathe in and breathe out. Use your senses. Get the feel of the place.'

He looked around, then leaned back in his seat and closed

his eyes. 'You're mad, you are.'

I opened my door. 'Okay. Remember what I said?'

'Stay here. Put my fingers in my ears.'

'I shouldn't be gone long.'

Like his brother's, Pete's house was a wide affair with a sweeping drive and a double garage, though his garden seemed neater and the atmosphere lacked the tension and edge that Little Jimmy's goons had created. The house was painted cream and rose up to a high gable, on the front of which was a security light. I counted three bedroom windows and there were probably a couple more round the back and a bathroom. Downstairs, it looked like a big sitting room on one side, maybe a dining room, another downstairs room of some kind and kitchen at the back.

Sam Dyke, architectural consultant to the hood.

Pete surprised me by answering his own door. His frame—not as big as his brother's, but impressive nonetheless—almost blocked the doorway. He wore his usual white tee-shirt and black jeans. A big belt buckle caught the morning sun and threw it back at me. He lifted his chin in recognition.

'You've got guts, Chief,' he said. 'Come in.'

He stepped back and I walked past him. A wide staircase rose straight ahead of me, with glass-panelled double doors on the left leading into a sitting room.

Pete had crossed the entrance and had bent down to talk to a wiry man in his thirties with a pink neck and cold eyes. He had the look of a man who could fillet you with a knife as easily as he could peel an orange with it. He stared at me while Pete talked in his ear, then nodded once. Pete turned back to me.

'This is Charlie,' Pete said. 'He works for me as a project manager. He's just leaving.' He said 'project' in the

Liverpudlian fashion – proe-ject.

Charlie levered himself forward and went past me without a word. The door closed behind him and the hall felt warmer at once.

The hall swept around the stairs and led into the kitchen at the back. For some reason, I felt I needed to know the layout of the house before I went any further. Pete saw me looking.

'Big, isn't it? I know what you're thinking—what's a knob-neck like me doing in a place like this? Simple answer, Chief—because I can afford it.'

'Good for you,' I said. 'Build it yourself, did you?'

'I know where you're going, so you can stop right there before it gets you into trouble.' He pointed to another door. 'Go through there. No, I didn't build it myself, so the walls are solid and it's not going to fall down next week. You think you've got my number because I'm a builder, don't you? Think I'm going to do everything on the cheap, ignore planning regs, bodge everything. You've got us all wrong.'

We'd gone through a door into an extension that thrust out into the garden. There were windows in the far wall so that you could look out into the garden if you wanted, but most of the walls were taken up with electronic equipment. It was Pete's games room. A fifty inch Panasonic plasma screen sat above the fireplace, while in the alcoves to either side there were various silver and black boxes on shelves. I made out a Sony Playstation 3, a hard-disk video recorder, what looked like a Philips music streaming box and some other equipment I didn't recognise. In the far corner were some weights and a static exercycle. A huge leather seat on a swivelling base pointed towards the television and a cabinet behind it contained about twenty different types of whisky.

'My play room,' Pete said. 'Where I was brought up we didn't really have time to play, or the space to do it in.'

'So you're making up for it.'

'Why not? I make a good living, I've got plenty of spare time on my hands. You're not one of these serious types are you? No time for fun and games.'

I turned to face him but made sure there was a space between us. 'I'm not here to talk about me, Pete.'

'Oh I know why you're here,' he said, opening a door that led outside. 'We'll talk outside.'

A patio of pale stone stretched the width of the house at the back, with a brick barbecue tucked into the corner. Beyond this patio, an extensive swathe of lawn led to elaborate flower beds and clusters of oak and chestnut trees. Scattered here and there amongst the flowers and trees were white statues of nymphs and mythological figures. At the bottom of the garden sat a summer house the size of a small Austrian chalet, and as I looked I saw Marie, Pete's tense wife, come out and lean on the balustrade, cigarette in hand. Today she'd changed from her pink jump-suit into a shiny blue-and-white track outfit, as though she were preparing to do a little light road training.

Pete had also lit up a Marlboro and blew the smoke sideways out of his mouth. His skin was sallow and pocked in the clear daylight. 'I don't know what you're up to,' he said, pointing his cigarette at me. 'I thought you might understand when a message was sent in your direction.'

'I don't like being told what to do and where to go,' I said. 'Your brother's got a few rocks in his head and I don't think you know what he's up to.'

'You leave me brother out of it,' he said, squaring his shoulders. 'You talk to him, you're talking to me. You can't play one of us off against the other, so quit it now.'

'You look tired, Pete. Are you sure you've got everything in hand? People never do what you want, do they?'

'What are you talking about?'

'I've come to tell you your brother's mixed up in something bigger than local graft.'

'Me brother? You're soft in the head, you are.'

'You know him. You know what he's capable of. I don't really care what else you're up to, but prostituting a girl against her will doesn't do either of you any favours.'

He looked away, into his garden, as though he found some solace there. 'You've got us all wrong, you have. We're honest builders doing an honest job. You leave us alone and we'll leave you alone.'

'Or what? Is that a threat?'

He shrugged, his massive arms lifting like boulders inside his tee-shirt. 'Take it how you want.'

'Then I'll take it as a threat.'

We stared at each other. Then he turned suddenly as he sensed Marie coming up behind him. 'Eh, love. You remember Mr Dyke?'

'Marie,' I said. 'You've got a nice house here. You must work hard.'

Pete laughed explosively. 'Wha'? Her? We've got an army of Poles does the housework and garden. All she has to do is pick out her next frock to wear at the Conservative Party dinner and dance.'

She looked up at him with something close to disgust in her face. 'I'm after making a cup of tea,' she said. 'Do you want one, Mr Dyke?'

'No, thanks. I'm on my way.'

She went inside, trailing a musty scent of cigarette smoke behind her.

Pete pointed at her back. 'Salt of the earth, that, man. Up

from nothing. Now look at the house she keeps.'

'I hope she can keep it,' I said. 'Family's important to you, isn't it? It is to me, too. I don't like it when my family gets dragged in to my work. I usually take steps to prevent it happening.'

'What's that mean? Is that a threat?'

'Take it how you want,' I said.

'Then I'll take it as a threat,' he said.

CHAPTER EIGHTEEN

Dan opened the door before I reached it.

'What did he say? Did he admit to anything?'

I started the car and headed home.

'He admits he's a bad man and he won't do it again. We shook hands and now we're blood brothers.'

Dan turned away and shook his head. 'I knew I wouldn't get a straight answer. Don't know why I bother.'

The lush scenery of the Wirral sped past. I thought about Pete and Little Jimmy and the rackets they had going that allowed them to live in this kind of opulence. Pete had been fairly straightforward with me but hadn't given anything away. He was obviously the brains of the two and was probably more conservative and cautious—Jimmy was younger, brasher, even more pumped on steroids and full of his own power. But they were loyal to each other. Pete wouldn't let me say anything about Jimmy, who in turn had deferred immediately to his brother at the point when he was about to carve me up. It would be difficult to turn them against each other.

On the other hand, they both had a lot to lose. Not only the set-up they had going in Liverpool, but the wealth and respectability that their success as builders was beginning to create for them. They were vulnerable.

What I didn't know yet was whether I was chasing down the right prey—I was yet to see any proof that they had anything to do with Kelly's disappearance. It was true that Jimmy had been the last person seen with her, but in her line of work that didn't necessarily mean anything.

Dan had been saying something while I was thinking. I turned to him. 'What did you say?'

'I said you've probably forgotten all about Kelly, haven't you?'

'Kelly who?'

'You can joke about it, but it's true. This has become a vendetta for you now. Your own little war.'

'You don't know what you're talking about.'

'They trashed your car, repainted your sitting room and worst of all, smashed your precious cds.'

'I'm so shallow.'

'Now you've forgotten what all this was about to begin with and you're just having a go at the biggest bullies in the playground.'

'That's what you think, is it?'

'So tell me I'm wrong.'

'You're wrong. That was easy. Ask me a hard one.'

'That's it, make fun. You're good at that. Never take anything seriously. Laura told me.'

'She did, did she?'

We were both quiet for a while. I didn't like him bringing Laura into the argument so easily. I'd told Pete to steer clear of my family, but it was strange to actually start thinking of the people in my life like that. I found myself feeling angrier than I'd been in a long while.

'You don't understand these people,' I said. 'I let you come along for the ride this time but don't get used to it. They would as soon rip your head off as look at you.'

'Dad, stay focused. You're letting them get their hooks in you.'

'Don't tell me what to do. I'll deal with them and I don't need a snot-nosed kid giving me advice. Where I come from you stand up for yourself or you've got no self-respect.'

I felt him staring at me. 'All right,' he said. 'Jesus, chill out.'

I felt a stab of guilt. I should have kept quiet. He was a teenager. It wasn't fair to let him see the anger that I usually kept hidden. It was useful to me sometimes, but I had to keep it in check or else it ruined things. Not even Laura had seen that side of me yet.

We were silent for a while, then he turned to me again.

'Tell me about her,' he said.

I knew who he meant immediately, and it flipped my stomach over. I thought of the first time I'd seen his mother, running down the stairs in the boarding house in Leeds where I'd just started living. Her hair bobbing up and down as she swished past me to drive off with a doctor parked at the kerb in an expensive German sports car.

And the last time I'd seen her, eighteen years later, curled up, suffocated, in the back of a 1973 Rolls-Royce Silver Shadow that was parked in a lock-up garage north of London.

I started to talk to him. At first the words were difficult to find, but after I'd been talking for a little while, they came easier. By the time I'd finished, I was drained, aware that finally I'd been able to deal with something that had been swimming in my subconscious for the last four months, since her death.

At last I could think about her without feeling guilty.

As we arrived back in Crewe I drove into a petrol station. 'Stay here,' I told Dan and climbed out. I filled the tank and observed the cars coming over the roundabout where the petrol station stood. I paid, then got back in. 'Watch that black Rover,' I said.

Dan sat up and turned to look out the rear window. 'What's going on?' he said.

'It's been with us for a few miles. Keep an eye on it.'

I drove off the forecourt and sped towards the centre of Crewe. There was little traffic so I saw the Rover appear in my rear view mirror immediately.

'He's coming,' Dan said.

Fifty yards ahead was another roundabout. I turned right, towards Sandbach, and picked up speed.

'He's keeping his distance but he's definitely following.'

'I've got him,' I said.

After another half mile there was a straight road without any parked cars. I drove for a hundred yards, then braked slowly and stopped. The Rover also slowed down. I started to reverse, then jammed on the brakes and leapt out of the car, running towards the black car and peering inside the windscreen.

The driver saw me easily and pulled out before I was close enough to see. As it went past me, the passenger held up his hand over his face and waved his fingers gently as the car went by.

Friendly, I thought.

CHAPTER NINETEEN

Later that afternoon I checked up on Ken Bullard again. I sat outside his house and after two hours and eleven minutes he turned up, limping down the street with a carrier bag of shopping in his hand. Whether he was a benefits cheat or not, at least he was consistent in his walking pattern. So far I had nothing to say against him and nothing to put in a report. Fifth law of detective school: be as persistent as you can afford to be. I could afford to give it another couple of weeks.

As I three-point-turned the courtesy car I saw the black Rover, which had been parked about thirty feet behind me. I waved at the driver and passenger as I went by, but they'd raised their hands to their faces so my gesture was lost on them.

The following day was an office day. I finalised the quarterly accounts and completed my VAT return, then photocopied it and stuck the official copy with a cheque into a post-box. As usual, I felt like a free man for at least another three months, so I walked back to the office and made a celebratory cup of coffee in the furniture store's kitchen.

When I climbed the stairs back to the office I looked out of my window and saw the Rover parked up and looking like a premonition of dark times ahead. Sooner or later I would need to talk to these jokers.

At five minutes to four, Laura rang my mobile.

'Where are you?' she asked.

'Still in the office. Paid my dues to Big Brother for another three months.'

'I don't know why you don't just get a book-keeper.'

'It keeps me on my toes, finance-wise. But this isn't why you rang.'

'Are we free tomorrow night?'

'For hang-gliding, water-skiing and sex. Possibly all three at the same time.'

'If you were good at one of them it would be helpful.'

'Whoa, there, cowgirl. Don't take advantage of my sunny mood. So what's happening tomorrow night?'

'Samantha from the office has asked whether we'd like to go over for a meal. Nothing fancy, just the four of us. You'll like her, she's nice.'

'Is she any good at hang-gliding, water-skiing or—'

'Don't go there, Beefy. I'll tell her that's a yes, then, shall I?'

'Mos def.'

She hung up. She didn't like it when I was hip and groovy.

The oak and silver birch trees bordering the lake rustled in the early evening air as Laura and I parked in Samantha's drive. Her house lay on the outskirts of Nantwich with a view of the lake where children and their parents sailed colourful dinghies and small boats in the summer months. In April it was still cool and the water on the reservoir patrolled back and forth in cold waves.

'Good view,' I said.

'She's lived here a few years,' Laura said, locking the car. 'She's traded up very cannily.'

I hadn't eaten all day in anticipation so I was first up the steps to ring the bell. Samantha was a sturdy woman in her early thirties. She let us in and introduced us to her partner, Damien, who waved cheerily from the kitchen while stirring a large pot. I put on my best middle-class behaviour as we walked through into the lounge and admired the garden, a new gazebo, the leather sofa from Ikea and the glasses in which cold gin and tonics were served. I felt myself beginning to sink into gentility as though I were being wrapped in a large, fur-lined overcoat that was quite nice for a short time but would soon become cloying and over-heated.

Given my state of mind, perhaps I shouldn't have agreed to come. It was pleasant enough to begin with. Samantha was attentive and friendly, and Damien had an Irish charm that Laura evidently found comfortable. Before long the three of them were laughing over the melon starter and Damien was telling us all about how he met Samantha at a Pilates class ... I put my nose in a glass of red wine and kept it there for an hour or so.

My thoughts kept returning to Pete Wilder standing in his garden, telling me in a subtle way that I'd been warned and I'd better stay warned. I wondered who he thought he was—someone whose neck was thicker than his head, telling me what to do, or else. Coming into my house and turning it into a child's play-pen. Which of course is exactly what they were—what all villains were, in the end. Kids who had no sense of limits and an inflated sense of their own importance. Sometimes you had to set limits, you had to be firm, even cruel ...

I realised Laura was staring at me across the table.

'What?' I said.

'You're muttering something, my love. Are you OK?'

Damien looked concerned. 'Will you take a spot of whiskey, Sam?'

I looked at them but I didn't recognise what I saw, their three faces turned towards me like bright pennies. White and black tee-shirts were swimming in front of me, filled out by testosterone-fuelled muscle and topped with balding ginger heads. Talking about clients who couldn't make up their minds whether to have the blue or the cream border around their newspaper adverts suddenly seemed the most stupid thing to be doing. I lurched to my feet, grabbing the table as I stood. Too much drink on an empty stomach, I realised. But I was well into it now.

'Sam?'

'Look,' I said, 'If the bloody client is giving you such a hard time, sack him. Get rid of him.'

'That's hardly—'

'You don't need to work with people who make life difficult for you,' I said. I'd backed away from the table, which seemed to be floating in the middle of the modish, genteel room, surrounded by abstract prints, stylish sound and television equipment, incense burners and silver-framed photos of the aged parents in Surrey. 'Find people you like and work with them,' I said dumbly. 'There are too many people out there who are bastards and want to hurt the things you love—the people you love. Leave them alone. Don't give them ammunition.'

'Sam, stop now.'

I found her face and held on to it with my eyes. It was the best thing I'd seen in a long while and I kept staring at it for what seemed a lifetime.

The air suddenly seemed cool. I looked around and I was standing outside, with Laura holding on to my arm. Somehow she'd managed to get her coat on.

'I'll drive,' I said.

'I don't think so,' she said, at the beginning of what was to be a long and difficult evening.

CHAPTER TWENTY

Surprisingly, Laura stayed with me that night. I woke with a rabbit's tongue in my mouth and a pile-driver trying to knock an exit through my skull, so I got out of bed, dressed quietly and went downstairs. I drank a litre of water and ate a piece of dry bread, then went outside into the garden.

It was Sunday morning, chill and expectant. The soil was hard and the rocks harder, but I'd timetabled today to make a start on a pond for my garden, so I fetched my spade and began digging.

An hour later, Laura appeared at the door. She looked at the hole I'd dug and raised her eyebrows.

'On the way to China?' she said.

'You can fill it in behind me,' I said. 'Then you won't have to show me to any of your friends.'

'If I still have any.'

'There is that.'

Now I knew she was awake I could start the really hard work. I had a few slabs and larger rocks that I began to attack and break up. She went inside and minutes later the smell of frying bacon turned my stomach inside out. A quarter of an hour later she opened the kitchen door again.

'Worker's breakfast,' she said. 'Bring your own tin mug.'

She'd laid out the table with bacon, egg, fried mushroom, baked beans and toast and marmalade to follow. My mouth watered as I washed my hands.

Afterwards, Laura said, 'So are you ready to say something now?'

'Do you mean like, Sorry for screwing up last night? That kind of thing?'

'Oh, that's just the start, big boy. I was thinking more in terms of an explanation of what's been going on behind your eyes for the last few days.'

I started to dry the pots that she'd been washing. I tried to reach back into what I was feeling, something I never found easy. Laura tried to help.

'Is it me?' she said. 'Do I make it difficult for you?'

'I'm the one who makes it difficult. I haven't been in this situation for years. Thinking about someone else. Two people, in fact. You and Dan. I seem to be guilty and irritated at the same time. No wonder I blew a fuse last night.'

'You were just drunk, Sam. You don't have to glorify it. You'd had nothing to eat all day and you drank too much too quickly.'

'It's never that simple. I can take a drink. I'm not one of your drunk private eyes, always drowning his sorrows.'

She didn't know what to say so she wiped the wooden table top and rinsed out the cloth. I watched the arc of her arms as she squeezed and laid out the cloth over the taps. The soft down on her forearms caught the morning light.

I went back outside and rolled out the Butyl rubber that was going to line the bottom of the pond. I cut it roughly to shape and laid it beside the hole, then ferried some moist sand over from where I'd dumped it and made a layer a couple of centimetres thick inside the hole. Now I placed the rubber lining in the hole and weighed down the edges with some of the stones I'd broken, then filled the lined cavity from a hose-pipe. The water level didn't sink once I turned off the water so I'd managed to get so far without spiking a hole in the lining. I was supposed to wait twenty-four hours now to see if there was a slow leak. I didn't know whether I had the patience.

Laura had come to the door to watch the final works. She held out a mug of coffee, which I took without looking at her.

She said, 'I've been thinking about your life problems.'

'Somebody has too. I don't seem to have too much success in that department.'

'I think it may be something to do with being a dad.'

'Keep talking, but do it slowly.'

'You've had no practice, have you? This young lad turns up and says you're his father and you're just not ready for it. Give yourself a break and while you're at it, stop being so hard on everyone around you.'

'That's all very well—'

'I know, it's not happening to me. But I'm not stupid. I'm actually quite an intelligent person, which you'd find out if you were to stop and talk to me for more than five minutes at a time.'

'It's like everything is running away from me. Out of my control.'

'And you do love your control. It must be a nightmare to have all these wild people trampling through your life.'

I looked at her. 'Oh, I can stand a little trampling from time to time. It's not all doom and gloom.'

'Be serious. The important thing is how you deal with it,

Sam. You've got to get a grip. You're acting as though something's eating away at you all the time.'

'I don't need the psychoanalysis, Laura.'

'You need something. You're not much fun at the moment. I didn't really sign up for this.'

I didn't like the direction the conversation was going all of a sudden. 'I've got to keep pushing,' I said. 'It's the only thing I know how to do. Like someone said, as you go through life your strength eventually becomes your weakness. It's the ability to recognise when one is turning into the other that marks out the wise man. Take out your stylus and write that down.'

She was sceptical of my mysticism. 'Be careful what you're pushing against. You don't know what might fall over.'

'I've never run away from a fight and I'm not going to stop now. If the Ginger Twins want to have a go, let them.'

Laura shook her head and turned away.

'You are crazy,' she muttered as she went indoors.

It's that thought that keeps me sane, I said to myself.

CHAPTER TWENTY-ONE

He hadn't told Mikey and Spud where he was going, but now he was in Manchester he wished they were with him. He didn't like the place. He didn't like Mancs—always whining, never happy, losers the lot of them.

He pointed the Corvette through the dark streets and turned up the CD player. Pink Floyd blasted out of the speakers—the digital remix of Dark Side of the Moon. 1973— what a great year. Aladdin Sane. Innervisions. For Your Pleasure ... absolute gold dust.

The car was a 2000 C5 in torch red with black leather seats, 5.7 litres rushing through his backside and up into his hands. Dual air-conditioner and twin airbags and switched to the Euro spec. He'd paid nearly twenty grand for it and loved it more than any other car he'd had. He thought about Kelly sitting in the passenger seat, looking trim and laughing. Hair grown out a bit more and her flicking it back from her eyes from time to time, then looking over at him and touching him on the knee. They'd be going somewhere up in the Lakes to one of those fancy hotels, spend the weekend looking in antique shops and perhaps him buying her a nice necklace or a dainty little bag to hang over her shoulder. He could almost taste what it would feel like when she was fixed up and not ragged round the edges, like she was now.

That's when he'd really start to live. Make the most of himself. Have done with Pete and set up on his own, a little outfit that would work online with a bit of enforcement thrown in. Keep a builder's yard perhaps as a front but not have Pete and his big ideas to cope with. South Africa — what a load of bollocks. They were doing well enough without going international. Pete had to be watched or he'd get them in trouble because he didn't know when to stop.

In the end he'd told Pete about Dyke. He was furious, of course, but they'd agreed to issue a warning. It usually worked, especially when the punter knew who the warning was from. There weren't many secrets between Jimmy and Pete and he hadn't liked not being square about Dyke. It nagged at him that he was keeping something from his brother. He wasn't used to it.

And then all that hassle with the police about that dead girl — that had really pissed Pete off. He should have put her somewhere else. In fact he'd nearly forgotten her. She was the first one, and it hadn't been good. Stupid bitch had just fought him all the way. He'd had to overdose her in the end just to get her to shut the fuck up. Pete hadn't known about her till the police came knocking at the door. There were some things Jimmy had had to keep quiet. Though he was beginning to see that it always came out in the end. That was a life lesson, as his old ma used to say.

And all that was why he hadn't told Pete the truth about Kelly. Pete asked whether Jimmy had let her go yet, and he didn't know why, but he'd said he had. Days ago, he'd said.

He knew it was stupid, but he couldn't admit to Pete that he still needed Kelly around. He didn't know what the fuck he was doing, if the truth be told. She just had something he wanted.

He had to bring his head back to the road now. Sparkle had told him where to park so his 'vette would be safe and where to go to do the business. Sparkle had sounded interested over the phone and Jimmy could tell he wanted to know what he was up to. But this was private. Pete didn't know. Mikey and Spud didn't know. It was party time for Jimmy and he was going to teach those bastards a lesson. Seeing how Kelly was suffering each day he held back her dose only increased his loathing. He had to make sure Pete never touched heroin in the business; he wouldn't stand for it.

The multi-storey was where Sparkle had said it would be and Jimmy put the car in a dark corner where it wouldn't be seen. There was even a man in the booth so Jimmy thought it would be pretty safe. He gave the man a hard stare as he went past so he'd remember the face if he had to. The man was in his fifties and didn't look up from his newspaper.

Jimmy came out into the cool air and pulled his collar up round his neck. He'd swapped his usual black tee-shirt for a Polartec fleece with a zip, then put a black leather jacket over the top. He took a blue Nike baseball cap out of his pocket and jammed it down as far as he could, then tugged the brim lower. He knew he was big but at least he wouldn't be recognised immediately.

A hundred yards ahead the road crossed a dark intersection where one of the traffic lights was broken. Jimmy took out his instructions and turned left, down a narrow street full of boarded-up shops. It was nearly eleven now and only a curry house and a fish-and-chip shop were open. Bored Indians stood behind the counters in both shops. Jimmy lowered his head and looked away. The smells from each shop hit the back of his throat and tasted sour. He hadn't eaten since lunch time and would kill a burger when he got home, but now he needed to be sharp.

It was a residential street with hedges and lamp-posts and black wheelie-bins parked in the front gardens. Two of the houses had skips full of house-bricks and timber standing on the road in front. More middle-class shits doing up their semis, he thought. Shouldn't complain, though—that was how he and Pete had started years ago. Buying up ramshackle properties round the corner from where they lived and breaking their arses to turn them round in less than a month, then selling them on. There was a time when students' parents would buy a house cheap and rent out the spare rooms not used by their own sprogs to pay for the mortgage. Then everyone and his uncle got on the bandwagon and you had to play underhand just to buy the properties—they were being sold before they'd even hit the estate agents' windows, so you had to grease a few palms to get a phone call before anyone else heard.

As he crossed in front of an alley between two houses, a shape moved. Jimmy stopped and turned, his senses wide open. He could tell it was a woman and he hoped she wasn't going to offer the usual. He took a step towards her and the shape resolved into a thin girl probably in her late twenties. Her face was round and pale and her hair stuck to her head as though she'd just stepped out of the shower. Jimmy looked her up and down. Thin but good body. Shuffling back and forth as she looked up the street, her hands in the pockets of an oversize man's coat. A small stud showing in her left nostril and a matching ones in her eyebrow. Jimmy hated that—all that body piercing.

Good. It made it easier.

'You after something, mate?' the girl asked, her voice hoarse, probably from cigarettes.

Jimmy took a step closer and she backed off.

'What you got?' he said. 'Is it you or something else?'

'Nah—not me, mate.' She held out a hand with a small silver wrap in it.

Jimmy thought she must be desperate to be so brazen, but that's why Sparkle had told him to come here. They were all desperate.

He looked up and down the street. A car had passed them and was turning the corner, and a couple of student-types with their baggy clothes had just crossed the street. Apart from that, no one was about.

'Not here,' he said to the girl. 'Go back.'

The girl looked up at him and for the first time realised how big he was. He laughed inside. It always surprised them when he got up close. It was a turn on.

But she was desperate for the money and went back into the dark. Jimmy followed her.

When she turned back to him he hit her once on the point of her nose. Her head snapped back and hit the wall behind, then she sagged. He caught her easily with one arm and let her rest there. She'd been knocked unconscious immediately and he thought he'd probably broken her nose. She was as light as the cashmere sweater he'd once bought for his mother. He never forgot the first time he'd touched that sweater and picked it up. It was like holding candy-floss.

He looked at the girl in his arms. Under the coat she was wearing a black tee-shirt like the ones he usually wore, though there were blood spots on it now. Her breathing was harsh, as though she were struggling to wake up. This close, he could see she wore a dark lip-stick and bits of blue eye-shadow on her lids. What was the point? He thought. I'm going out to do a bit of drug-pushing, so I'll put on a bit of lippy ...

Her body rose and fell in his arms. He thought he could just reach out a hand and feel her up. Even put his hand up her shirt and get a good one, while she was out. Then he felt ashamed. That wasn't what he was here for. That was just crude.

He noticed that her stash was in a bag looped round her waist. He reached down and undid the zip, then pried out half a dozen wraps, stuffing them in the pockets of his own jacket. It was as though this was a worse indignity because she began to struggle then and opened her eyes with a flutter.

Jimmy took a tighter grip of her, looping his left arm around and gripping her so that she couldn't move. She didn't struggle but looked up at him with wide, calm eyes. Then he reached into his jacket pocket again and took out his cutters.

CHAPTER TWENTY-TWO

The next morning I took a call from Trevor Clarke.

'It's on the website this morning,' he said.

'Back up a couple of steps.'

'The Liverpool council news website. The permission at the Dorset Estate has been granted to Wilder Shores—they're going to be able to build their cardboard boxes, so long as they put in a roundabout and meet a couple of other minor conditions. I'm going out to interview the head of the protest group. Thought you might like to know.'

'The Wilders are going to be busy boys.'

'Oh they'll sub-contract like crazy. Every chippie and sparks in the area will be rubbing their hands together. Christmas time.'

He sounded happy. I couldn't square it with the cynical hack I'd met in the cafe in Aigburth. I said, 'I thought you wanted the Wilders to lose. Sounds to me like you've swallowed a jumping-jack.'

'It's news, boy! News! Drama, tension, lives in the balance ... All that stuff. Especially after they were in the headlines not long since. Their profile's going to be higher than they want, which means they're going to be looked at a lot harder than they're used to as a couple of jobbing builders.'

When he hung up, I navigated to the Liverpool council website and found the news page. It was the topmost item, entered that morning. It was brief and pithy, almost as though the PR flak had had vinegar in his mouth when he wrote the text. The words 'controversial' and 'protest' were prominent in the story, but nothing was said about the Wilder brothers, who were masked behind their corporate name. A 'spokesman' said they were 'very pleased' to have been awarded the contract, a new development of some fifteen executive houses, built to the highest specs. I could see them already—square front, double garage, a short drive of creamy pea-shell leading up to the door, a patch of green lawn in front and a larger oblong at the back surrounded by six-foot high orange fencing panels. Four bedrooms, one master with en suite, separate bathroom upstairs and one inside the front door downstairs. Modern kitchen with a tall Smeg fridge. Television point in every room. For the thrusting executive with regulation blonde wife and 2.4 articulate kids who would join myspace before they were eight years old and probably keep a pony on a farm and have dancing and piano lessons until they reached grade four, at which point they would rebel and take up something more dangerous, like golf.

I rang a contact number but got nowhere. In my experience it's easier to see people in person than worm your way through telephone gate-keepers, so I climbed in the navy-blue Astra and drove to Liverpool again. The car was racking up the miles and I'd probably have a hefty surcharge to pay when I handed it back.

I'd taken the address of Addison's office from his

secretariat when I phoned in the guise of Joe Gorman, concerned resident. The office turned out to be located in one of the old Victorian fortresses a stone's throw from the Liver building and in sight of the river. An information plaque in the foyer directed me to the fourth floor, which was laid with polished tiles and decorated with standard public bureaucracy cream walls, on which hung several aerial photos of Interesting Places to See in Liverpool. I recognised Albert Dock and Anfield football ground, but that was it. A wooden stand held several dozen flyers and pamphlets of even more Places to See.

A glass door was marked Reception, and behind it was a small room inhabited by a woman in her forties with trim red hair and a business-like dark suit. I pressed my Charm button before I spoke, and explained that I would like to see Mr Addison if that would be at all possible.

'And you are?'

'My name's Sam Dyke, and no, I don't have an appointment.'

She smiled but I could tell she didn't mean it. 'He's got wall-to-wall meetings this afternoon,' she said. 'Where did you say you were from?'

'Never mind,' I said, and left.

In the corridor there were a couple of hard chairs. I settled myself in to wait, wondering if there really was a connection between the Wilder brothers and a respectable, probably middle-aged Planning Manager who had a lot to lose if any wrong-doing was proved.

At twelve-thirty exactly the door of Reception opened and two secretaries came out, giggling with each other and opening cigarette packets as if they couldn't even wait to get outside the building. They were followed by a tall, haggard-looking man with a hooked nose and wearing black-rimmed glasses. He was probably in his late thirties though his receding hairline made him look older. I took a chance and as he passed me I said, 'Mr Addison?'

Bingo. He turned to me with a mild frown. 'Yes?'

I walked up close to him. Sometimes a little intimidation can help. 'What happened with the Dorset Estate?' I asked. 'How come the permission was granted so easily?'

'Who are you?'

'An interested party. I've looked at the information on your website, and the local development plan for the Dorset Estate area has already been met. You planned for three thousand new houses in that area in the period up to the beginning of this year. Now you're adding more when you don't need to.'

'If you looked at the plan more closely, Mr Whoever-you-are, you'd see that we have a commitment to provide as much low-cost housing as is concomitant with the needs of the community and the preservation of greenfield sites.'

'Executive housing isn't low-cost housing. And the community say they don't need this estate because they'd rather have the green field. You're just rolling over for the developers, aren't you?'

He was getting red-faced and a nerve pulsed under his left eye. He had a prominent mole on his upper lip that he now touched with the end of his tongue, as if for comfort. 'I don't know the Wilder brothers,' he said, 'and I have no intention of either meeting them or continuing this conversation, which is completely unacceptable. If you don't leave right now I shall call the police.'

I stepped back. 'I never mentioned the Wilder brothers,' I said. 'Nice of you to bring them into the conversation.'

He wasn't fazed. 'It would be odd if I wasn't familiar with the names of the important developers in the city.' He smiled grimly. 'Now push off, before I get the police to twist your arm.'

'You say you don't know them, but I'm damn sure they know you. This isn't finished, Addison. You can tell them that from me the next time you see them.'

I walked past him and went down the stairs, feeling more self-important than was good for me.

Trevor Clarke answered his mobile on the second ring.

'How's it going with the disgruntled residents?' I asked.

'That you, Dyke? They're organising a meeting for tomorrow night. And they want to publish a letter in my rag deploring the whole sorry incident ... Blah blah blah. The Wilders have got a fight on their hands, that's for sure.'

'Can we meet? I'm in town.'

'I'm on my way back anyway.'

He described a coffee house around the corner from where I was standing, so I walked up there and waited the twenty five minutes it took him to drive back, park and walk the two hundred yards from his office.

'I went to see Patrick Addison,' I said when he'd sat down.

'Did he actually see you, or did he run away and hide like he normally does?'

'I trapped him with a cunning plan. He wasn't particularly happy to talk.'

'He never is. He hides behind the bureaucracy. Anyone would think he was a high-court judge rather than a journeyman public servant. But I'd watch out if I were you. The position he's in, he's likely to have some high-placed friends. And things being the way we think they are, they might owe him a favour.'

He took an old green tobacco tin from his pocket and

began rolling a thin cigarette.

I said, 'Have the police said anything yet about the girl's body I found?'

'Gina Lamont,' he said. 'Went missing in Manchester a couple of months ago. Traced her through dental records. Her parents hadn't reported her missing, which I suppose tells you something about the level of communication between them.'

'Anything else?'

He looked at me through the blue smoke of his cigarette. 'I do have a day job, you know.'

'Someone told me this is news—drama, tension, lives-in-the-balance, that kind of stuff.'

'Is this the way you grill your interviewees? Take the piss out of them?'

'You use whatever language is appropriate. Shall I start again?'

He turned his chair sideways, as though making a point. 'Poor old Gina Lamont seems to have been a waif and stray. They don't know much about her except she was probably living on the streets.' He stopped and looked at me closely again. 'Why are you so interested in her anyway? It looks like she was just a junkie dumped on a building site that happened to be owned by the Wilders. Even they wouldn't be so stupid as to leave her on their own property. So why the interest?'

I hesitated. I didn't know how much I wanted to tell Clarke about Kelly and Dan and the original reason behind this whole case. On the other hand, with his contacts in Liverpool, he could be useful.

'I'm looking for a missing person,' I said.

'I'm guessing from your reaction that this wasn't her.'

'No. How old was Gina?'

'Twenty. Pretty thing, and from a good family. I bet they regret not talking to her more, now.'

'You got any kids?'

'Not that I'll admit to. Divorced fifteen years ago, without issue, as they say. I don't know whether I was firing blanks or the old lady was a fallow field. God knows we had enough practice. I know you wouldn't think it to look at me now, but I was a pretty good swordsman in my day.'

This was beyond the bounds of what I needed to know about him, so I drew the conversation to a rapid close and left. When I looked back he was sitting cross-legged in his chair, looking into the distance and taking hefty draws on his cigarette as though he were on the observation deck of a cruise liner watching a fine sunset.

It was a shame to waste my time in Liverpool so I headed out to the corporate headquarters of Wilder Shores—the warehouse up in the docks. Rain was sleeting in from the Mersey as I parked in the street and hunkered down. I was in luck, because I could see Little Jimmy's Corvette parked directly outside the entrance to the building. I'd stocked the car with some cds I'd rescued from the house, and I put Steely Dan's Countdown to Ecstasy in the player and lay back to listen to Skunk Baxter rip the guts out of Bodhisattva.

Rain slithered down the windscreen of the Astra, but it didn't prevent me from identifying the younger of the Wilder twins as he came out of his office half-way through Show-Biz Kids. I put the car in gear and followed as he roared away, the twin exhausts rippling the air behind him. Fortunately he wouldn't recognise my car because he thought I drove a red Cavalier.

We drove parallel to the Mersey, buffeted by the wind and rain sweeping in from the Irish sea. The sky was like a dull charcoal sketch and all the colour had been sucked out of the city, leaving it wintry and grey and as lifeless as a cemetery. Eventually we turned into the town and headed towards Sefton Park. Jimmy knew where he was going and drove confidently through Aigburth until he turned down Lark Lane and found a parking space. I drove past and pulled into another space further down, then turned in my seat and watched Jimmy climb out and walk into a small café, ignoring the rain that bounced off his shoulders and ran down his head.

The café was too small for me to make a discreet entrance, so instead I ran across the road and walked along the pavement, stopping occasionally to look in windows in case Jimmy came out without warning. Eventually I came to the café and stopped briefly to peer through the menus and advertising flyers stuck on the entrance door. There were half a dozen people scattered amongst the tables, and Little Jimmy and Patrick Addison were sitting in the furthest corner, almost hidden. Addison was bent urgently over the table, making a point by stabbing a finger into the plastic top so hard that from where I was standing I could see his tea-cup wobble. Little Jimmy reached out a leisurely hand and held the cup stable but didn't seem to be saying anything.

Back in my car I turned the heater on to de-mist the windows, then sat and waited. After five minutes the rain stopped and I cracked a window. Eleven minutes later, the front door of the cafe opened and Addison came out. I lifted my Canon EOS camera with the 11x zoom and took a 3-second burst of photos. A few minutes later, as I expected, Little Jimmy came out too—he didn't have the patience to wait longer. He was framed and caught in pixels looking around him briefly, then walking confidently back to his monster car. I wondered what he thought about Addison's agitation. And I wondered why Addison was agitated, though I hoped my presence in his face earlier in the day had something to do with it.

CHAPTER TWENTY-THREE

Only when I arrived home and turned on my mobile again did I find that Trevor Clarke had left me a voice mail. He'd been told that the previous evening two drug pushers from one of the seedier parts of Manchester had been admitted to hospital.

'Wait for this,' Clarke said. 'They'd both had two fingers snipped off their right hand. Guess whose calling card that is? You ask me, Little Jimmy is cracking up. He's barmy if he thinks people won't know who it is. And Dyke, don't call me back because I don't have any more details yet. I'll let you know.'

I made myself a coffee and thought about what Clarke had told me. He was right that people would know it was Little Jimmy who was responsible for maiming the two victims. What I didn't understand was why he was targeting drug pushers all of a sudden. It seemed like a minor activity for someone who was apparently involved in more serious criminality. Perhaps he was just having a little fun, indulging himself while he still could, before his other business got too all-consuming. After all, judging from the cabinet in his workroom, it did seem that snipping off people's fingers was a hobby.

I'd been ignoring Laura, so I bought some flowers and arranged to pick her up from work and take her for a meal. She sounded surprised but pleased. Sam Dyke, romantic warrior.

As usual, we ended up at a curry house down the road from the railway station in Crewe. They knew us there and gave us a nice table away from the flat-screen TV that showed endless clips from Bollywood films—with gently throbbing soundtrack—so neither of us could be distracted by the bright colours or dazzling scenery. It was an innovation introduced by the owner but the staff knew it irritated most of the customers.

I brought Laura up to speed with the Wilder twins. I'd decided it was easier to include her than try to protect her by saying nothing. If I kept quiet about what I was doing she just grew worried. She might still be worried but at least she knew what she was worried about.

'So on the one hand, Jimmy's presenting the front of a successful builder, while on the other hand, pardon the pun, he's creeping round the backstreets of Liverpool snipping off people's digits. What kind of creature is that?'

'Someone with a very narrow view of human beings,' I said.

'And what can you do about it?'

'Nothing yet. It's all speculation and surmise at the moment. I have to wait till I find evidence.'

The popadums came and we ate in silence for a while— or as silently as you can when crunching popadums. Then I told her about meeting Addison, the planner.

'And did he act guilty, as they say? Whatever the hell that looks like?'

'He has a little mole on his upper lip — on that bit between the bottom of your nose and the bow of your top lip, what do you call it?'

'Something Latin, like septum or patella. But not those.'

'Whatever it's called, he touches it with his tongue. Like a salamander or something. I'd bet a psychologist would have a field day with it.'

'They call it "leakage". When your body language gives away what you might be thinking or feeling.'

'He was angry at me for even daring to bring up the question of the Dorset Estate. But he was anxious, too. And then when I saw him in the café with Jimmy he was certainly making a point. He's not happy. I think we've begun to make a dent in their cute little game.'

The waiter brought my rogan josh and Laura's dhansak. The heavy tomato aroma hit the back of my throat before I tasted the food.

'So what's your next step? Do you carry on watching Addison to see what he does?'

'You have to watch the main players. That's the Wilder brothers, and probably Jimmy more than Pete. He seems to be the one with the least sense of restraint.'

She nodded and sipped her water. 'Sam, I can't help thinking this is taking you away from what Dan asked you to do. You were supposed to be looking for this girl, not bringing down a crime syndicate, however pathetic they sound.'

First Dan, now Laura. Both of them suggesting that I'd lost sight of the original case. It was beginning to irritate me that they thought I didn't know what I was doing. I put down my fork.

'Laura, a case like this isn't a single thread. You don't just follow a string of clues and find the answer at the end. What am I supposed to do, burst into Jimmy's house and turn it upside down looking for Kelly? She could be anywhere, and not necessarily in the house. You have to sit back and gather some data.'

'Have you considered what's going on for Dan while you're "gathering data"?'

'That's between me and him. I'll talk to him.' I put my hand over hers on the table. 'A lot of what I do is just like shaking a tree till the soft fruit falls off. I sit and I watch until it seems like it's ready to fall, then I give the trunk a good old kick and see what happens. I don't really want to push the twins any further because it might put Kelly in more danger. Assuming she's still alive.'

'Are you hopeful?'

'I have to be. Otherwise I'd just give up, wouldn't I?'

CHAPTER TWENTY-FOUR

I was outside Little Jimmy's house by 7.30 the next morning. At that time the drive had been clear and trouble free. I didn't think the Wilders would be early risers, and I was right. It was 8.45 before the curtains on one of the windows drew back and Jimmy's large chest appeared at an upstairs window. Forty-five minutes later, his two henchmen drove up to the gated entrance and were allowed in.

Then nothing happened for two hours. I wondered what Jimmy and his partners did all day. They certainly weren't holding important meetings with town planners or suppliers of construction materials. Maybe Jimmy let Pete do all that heavy lifting—he seemed to be the one with the brains, after all. Perhaps they were watching re-runs of the Sopranos, or playing Grand Theft Auto on the X-Box. I began to wonder whether watching the front of a house was all my life held in store for me over the next couple of weeks. The exciting life of a private investigator was enough to make your pulse race.

That'll teach me to get bored. The car door was wrenched

open suddenly and a large pair of hands grabbed my arm and pulled me out. It was a familiar feeling. I should learn to lock doors.

Two men in short jackets and matching stone faces each seized an arm and pushed it up behind me. I was forced to lean forward as they marched me away, towards a midnight blue Peugeot Boxer that was parked thirty yards behind us. As we approached the side door slid open and I was pushed up and in.

One of the pair of bullies got in with me and said, 'Sit down. You're not going to get hurt.'

The other slid the door shut and I watched through the windscreen as he walked to my car, got in and started the engine. When it was running, our vehicle started up and drove past it. I turned and watched as my car fell into place behind me.

'I was quite happy where I was,' I said.

'You're up for a meeting. Just sit quiet and you'll be OK.'

'Meeting who?'

The man didn't answer me. Perhaps he didn't like my grammar. Instead he turned to look through the front window as we headed towards the motorway. He was about thirty-five and looked fit. He had short hair and the tight skin of someone who kept himself in training. He'd leaped easily into the Boxer and his grip on my arm had been more firm than was necessary. The driver of the car also had that burnished look of someone who knew how to handle himself.

Interesting, I thought to myself. Some kind of special operations—military or specialised police unit. The fact that they were bringing my car suggested I was going to be taken for some time rather than just hauled off for a brief bout of questioning. I moved around in my seat and made myself comfortable.

We drove out of Liverpool and headed into Manchester in mid-morning traffic. We passed the blue tower blocks of Salford Quays and went on into the centre of town, turning up past the Bridgewater Hall and G-Mex and heading north. I considered leaping out of the car—but then what? A mad chase through crowded shops? Old-age pensioners up-ended as I thrust them aside? Have-a-go youths hurling themselves in front of me like American football linebackers?

Instead, I took a deep breath and absorbed as many details of my kidnappers as I could. At least it kept my brain occupied.

Eventually we pulled up in front of an anonymous concrete building with reflective blue windows. The door slid open and I was pulled on to the pavement and then up a short path and into a dark foyer. There was an unoccupied reception desk and a low table at the centre of a group of plush seats. It was like the ante-room to an expensive private clinic, without the smell of antiseptic. I could hear voices from down a corridor but there was no one in sight.

My arm was tugged again and we walked down a different corridor, past a row of numbered doors. We halted in front of number 8 and the door was opened for me.

'Take a seat,' said my host. 'Enjoy the view.'

The door closed behind me. I was in what appeared to be an interview room containing a plain table and three plastic chairs. The view outside the window turned out to be the Rochdale Canal, weaving its sluggish way north out of the town and heading towards Oldham. I watched as a group of boys wandered down the tow-path chucking stones at the water just to see it break.

Fifteen minutes later the door opened and two men

entered. The first was the one who'd come with me in the back of the Boxer. The other was a tall man with a casual air but a few more years on the clock. He wore a brown tie that matched his jacket and a pair of tan brogues. His hair was close cropped but still showed a deep black without any grey. He pointed me to a chair and sat opposite me when I took it. His younger colleague stood behind me in a classic intimidation set up. The man facing me across the table glanced at the canal briefly but then dismissed whatever it was he saw there.

'My name's Moody,' he said. 'And you're Sam Dyke. So that's the introductions out of the way. I like to sort out the pleasantries first.'

'I admire a polite copper. Shows respect.'

'So perhaps you can tell me what the fuck you were doing watching that scumbag Jimmy Wilder.'

'Are you allowed to call people scumbags?'

'I can call him what I like. Answer the question.'

He had folded his hands calmly on the table. There are times in this job when you know you have to give something to get something, and I guessed that Moody was someone who knew that game as well as I did.

'You go first,' I said. 'What is this set-up? SOCA? You weren't watching me to see what I was doing. You were watching Jimmy and you found me in the crosshairs.'

Moody looked at me with eyes that didn't waver but I could tell he was thinking. If he knew who I was and what I did, he'd probably take a risk. My reputation wasn't that bad with the local fuzz. On the other hand, he held all the cards and didn't need to tell me anything he didn't want to. If he *was* from the Serious Organised Crime Agency, he could pretty much do what he wanted.

'The Wilder brothers are pieces of shit,' he said. 'They

intimidate, threaten, bully and generally throw their weight around. They also build crap houses, a circumstance that seems to have slipped past the various planning officers they've come into contact with over the last few years.'

'Okay, I changed my mind – you're the SWAT squad for the Building Association. He Who Builds, Wins.'

'Never mind who I am. The point is, you look like you're going to gum up our works here. Even Jimmy's not so dumb as to miss you squatting on his doorstep.'

'We've already had that discussion.'

Moody looked over my shoulder at his colleague, then back at me. If he was surprised that I'd already spoken to Jimmy, he didn't show it. 'So you've got a permit, or what? Did he take a shine to you?'

'We agreed to disagree on one or two particulars. His brother tried to put me right as well.'

I liked winding Moody up. I hate it when people act as though they know what I'm thinking.

'Now I am intrigued,' Moody said. 'You've been in their faces and you're still standing to tell the tale.'

'I can be very diplomatic.'

Moody stared at me for a little while. Like his men, he seemed lithe and fit and his eyes were clear. 'So what's your story?' he asked.

'I don't have to say anything to you. Especially with the way you send out your invitations.'

'I don't have time for this, Dyke. You're a low-rent investigator who's landed smack in the middle of an ongoing project, so I need to know who's put you there. Your type don't usually work for free, so I'm assuming you have a client.'

'I couldn't possibly say.'

'Look, my days are long and tedious enough without you

making my life more difficult. Play by the rules and we can be friendly about this. Otherwise I might have to pull rank.'

'You do what you like.'

'Give me a bone, Dyke, so I don't have to put you away until we've finished. And believe me, I can do that.'

The room was so quiet I thought it was probably sound-proofed. There was no noise from the rest of the building or from the canal-side beyond the window. I leaned forward and my chair creaked like a mighty oak falling to earth.

'The residents committee for the Dorset Estate area have retained me to look into the Wilders. They were hoping I could get some evidence that would halt the progress of the planning application.'

'That's already been granted. So why are you still hanging around Jimmy Wilder?'

I shrugged. 'It's a battle lost, not the war. Come on, Moody. You know the Wilders. Just because they're respectable at one level doesn't mean they can keep their act clean.'

'What do you know?'

'You first.'

Moody had leaned forward in his chair to match me. Now he leaned back again and glanced at his colleague behind my shoulder. 'Look what we've got here, Simms.'

'What's that, sir?'

'A perfect example of what happens when you start thinking you're bigger than your job.'

I said, 'What's that supposed to mean?'

'While you were being brought in I did some research. Found out all about your previous life in Customs and Excise. Hot shot investigator, pressed all the right buttons, climbing that career ladder hand over fist. Until they found some irregularities and started investigating your unit. Then you clammed up.'

'No charges were pressed against me.'

'There's no smoke without fire in this life, Dyke.'

'I'm glad to see you're upholding the force's reputation for original thinking.'

He smiled grimly. 'I'm no fool, you know. I can read between the lines. Just because a couple of men in your unit were sent down for openly stupid corruption doesn't mean that you're implicated. But the way you handled yourself during the investigation got right up some people's noses. I talked to one of them. "Self-righteous prick" was I think one of the politer phrases used. I'm beginning to see what he meant.'

'I've always brought out the best in people.'

'I don't believe you're crooked, but I don't believe you're telling me the truth, either. You're probably just protecting your client. I'd probably do the same.'

'Aren't we two noble fellows?'

'So I'm going to let you go and do what you have to do, but with a caveat that you watch yourself. Wherever you are, we'll know.'

'Does that mean the black Rover is going to carry on keeping me company?'

'You won't see us again.'

That didn't really answer the question but I wasn't going to push it. He still hadn't told me what his interest in the Wilder brothers was. It was worth a try.

'So I don't make any stupid mistakes,' I said, 'why don't you tell me why you're watching the Wilders?'

'Just make sure our project doesn't go pear-shaped because of anything you do. Simms, give him his keys.'

The keys landed with a clatter on the table in front of me. Moody stood up and took out a business card from a small silver box. He flipped it on to the table. There was nothing but a name and a telephone number. No address, no rank, no divisional name.

'Call me if you want to talk. I'm all ears.'

He walked out of the room and Simms tapped me on the shoulder. 'Out.'

I turned and gave him a withering stare. I said, 'You do go on, don't you?'

CHAPTER TWENTY-FIVE

My car was waiting on the road outside. I drove home and went for a run to get rid of my frustration. I didn't have any difficulty with authority—so long as it wasn't directed at me. If it was, I became consumed with a raging sense of injustice that could only be dealt with by doing something active. Usually this meant hitting someone.

I ran a couple of laps around the field behind my house, then climbed over the stile and ran five road miles out into the country and back. Traffic was light after lunch so I was able to think about what I knew so far without fear of being run down because I wasn't paying attention.

First, I didn't know any more about Kelly's whereabouts than I did a week ago. I wondered whether she was still alive, and if she was, what kind of condition she was in. Was she getting the drugs she needed to stay sane? Was she still in the country? Or had her kidnapper got rid of her— perhaps sold her abroad? In the same way that Eastern European girls had been heading westwards in the last ten years, usually to work in hotels as cleaners or waitresses, likewise there was a trade in the opposite direction for well-fed capitalist honeys. I didn't know whether the Wilder brothers were involved in the flesh trade or not. I liked to think they were because it fitted my view of their amoral tendencies, but I had no evidence beyond the word of a prostitute who'd seen Kelly with Little Jimmy. That was one incident, without corroboration. I had no hard evidence despite my stake-outs.

What I was also aware of, though, was the Wilder brothers' utter shamelessness about their violence. They walked around like a couple of prize-fighters, arms akimbo, legs shuttling back and forth like tree trunks on the move. Their physical presence was an act of intimidation. They didn't actually need to beat people up any more. It was like the bully at school who demonstrates his power on a couple of weaker pupils and then doesn't have to do anything for the rest of his educational career—the threat is enough to get his own way.

And when I thought about them in relation to Dan and Laura, I broke out in a cold sweat. Dan had no real idea how brutal the Wilders could be. And Laura hadn't asked to be involved in this situation. Sometimes with clients it got personal—they might become friendly with you and begin to treat you as one of the family. It was as though the fact that you'd helped them in a particularly difficult time of their lives made them want to thank you by treating you as more than the hired help. With the Wilders, though, everything was personal. They weren't my clients, obviously, but they didn't seem to mind insinuating themselves into my life through intimidation and threats. If I'd put Laura or Dan in jeopardy because of my own self-importance, I'd never forgive myself.

The house phone was ringing when I got home.

'Dad, it's me.'

'Hey. I was just thinking about you.'

There was a pause in which I could hear the kind of background noise I'd normally associate with a busy office — chatter, telephones ringing, bursts of laughter. Dan soon dispelled that idea.

'I've been arrested,' he said.

I took that in. I heard his breathing on the other end of the line.

I said the stupid thing you say in this situation: 'What for?'

'They think I had something to do with Kelly's disappearance. They think I killed her.'

I pay for legal services from a practice in Manchester, so forty minutes after I arrived at the station in Crewe where Dan was being held, my solicitor, Veronica, strode into the lobby, her long mane of crinkly hair flying behind her. She saw me sitting against a wall and came over.

'I didn't even know you had a son,' she said, unable to stop herself from grinning. 'Secrets and lies, Mr Dyke, secrets and lies.'

'A long story,' I said. 'What can we do?'

'You can sit here while I go and ask a few questions.' Then she smiled. 'Don't worry, Sam. I'll see he's OK. They don't even have a body yet, do they? It's a fishing expedition.'

She went back to the desk and started talking in a low voice to the custody officer. A few minutes later she came back.

'OK, they're getting ready to take him to the Custody Suite in Macclesfield. I've insisted that I see him, but they won't let you in. He's not a minor any more so you don't have a right to see him. You'll get an opportunity later.'

'Should I go to Macclesfield with him?'

'You'll spend a lot of time hanging around. I'd wait until I get a clearer picture of what's happening. They'll probably only hold him for twenty four hours anyway — as you know.'

A few months before, Veronica had helped me when I'd been held on suspicion of murder. She knew I knew the drill.

The custody officer called Veronica's name and she hurried off. I sat still for two minutes, then got up and left.

I felt powerless and angry but couldn't do anything — always a potent combination for me. I phoned Laura and told her what had happened, then I wandered around, looking in shop windows, until I saw Veronica coming out of the building half an hour later.

'How is he?'

'He's having a fine time. He's insisting on all his rights, the little cowboy. He didn't say anything to them until I arrived, and then he told them that on the advice of his solicitor he wasn't going to say anything. Really cheesed them off.'

'Problems with authority,' I said. 'I wonder where he gets that from. So what's next?'

'Well they're just waiting for transport to arrive to take him to Macclesfield, where they'll question him again. I can't really see what the case is, apart from the fact that he didn't report her missing for a few days. He tells me he's got you working on it.'

'I specialise in freebies. When your only child asks you to help find his disappeared junkie prostitute girlfriend, what are you going to do?'

'I see where you're coming from and I feel your pain. Incidentally, he asked me to tell you to find someone called Pedlar John. He's not seen him for a while and thinks he might be able to help.'

'I doubt it, but I'll see what I can do.'

'Look, there's the custody van arriving. I'll talk to you later.'

She reached up to give me a peck on the cheek then turned on a heel and left.

I went back to my car and pulled out the card that Moody had given me. I dialled his number on my mobile phone. It was answered on the second ring.

'Moody, it's Sam Dyke.'

'I wondered if you'd call.'

'What do you know?'

'Not much more than you. The name of your son was tagged and when it hit a trigger I was kept in the loop. We're very efficient nowadays, you know.'

'Did you have anything to do with his arrest?'

'Watch what you're saying, Dyke.'

'If I find out you had him put away to warn me off—'

'You'll do what, exactly?' His leisurely drawl had become even more elongated.

'Just keep off my back.'

'If it's any consolation, Dyke, I had nothing to do with your little boy's arrest. I do have rather more important things on my desk than ruining your day, fun though that would be.'

I cut the connection before I said anything both of us would regret.

CHAPTER TWENTY-SIX

On the doorstep he'd felt OK. Now he's inside he's feeling twittery. He isn't used to being treated well by Pete—it doesn't feel right.

Still, now he's sitting comfortably, in the big lounge. Plasma screen TV hanging on the wall, size of a pool table, soft sofas, loads of electronic toys. He wonders how many of them were nicked. But he doesn't say anything. You don't challenge Pete Wilder unless you want him to turn you over to Little Jimmy.

Marie out in the kitchen somewhere, making tea, watching Richard and Judy on a drop-down screen. This is the life. Nice house, money coming in, woman making you something to eat. Which reminds him, he's hungry. But he's always hungry. He never gets enough to eat, which is why he's so scrawny.

'Cup of tea?' Pete asks him.

'That'd be boss,' he says. 'Any chance of a biscuit?'

Pete looks at him sideways. 'Might be able to rustle up a piece of lemon cake if you want.'

'Always find room for that.'

Pete goes to a hatch in the wall and leans through to talk to Marie. Pedlar John looks through the floor-length windows at the end of the room. Garden just coming on, with it being the end of April. He always thought he'd like a garden, muck around with flowers and shrubs and so forth. Didn't know anything about it, really, but how hard could it be? Stick them in the ground and watch them push up. He quite liked that idea, being an old man pottering around, a shed at the bottom with lots of green tools inside and boxes of chemicals ...

He realises Pete is sitting opposite him and has said something.

'What?' he says. 'I was day-dreaming, Pete. Sorry.'

Pete shaking his head. 'Bad habit, Chief, bad habit. Got to be alert.'

'Your country needs lerts!'

'John, calm down. Take a deep breath. I understand this is probably weird for you. You're a cheap scrounger with a few contacts, and here you are in my front room, drinking my tea and getting my sofa mucky.'

'These are clean trousers, Pete. I changed specially.'

'Just listen up.'

'Sorry, Pete.'

'What do you know about this Sam Dyke character?'

'Not a lot. He's my mate's dad, as you know. Thinks of himself as a tough guy.'

'What do you think his game is?'

Pedlar John leans back on the sofa, thinking. He's in a horrible position—and it's all his own fault. Thought he was doing his mate Dan a favour and the next thing he gets a call from the Wilders. Shit starting to rise above his ears already. He should have just left it all alone.

But he knows the Twins have already sent a message to Dyke, probably using that psycho Charlie and a couple of his mates. So what's this about? What do they expect him to know that's any different?

'Not a hard question, John. An answer today would be helpful.'

'Sorry, Pete. I'm just trying to work out what you're after. As I understand it you've already had words with Dyke and let him know where you stand. He's stupid if he carries on fishing, isn't he?'

'You're answering the wrong question. I'll do the thinking here, if that's all right. I daresay you think you're a cunning little monkey, but actually you're a piece of shit I'm likely to wipe off my shoe any minute, so don't go all clever on me.'

His left leg starts to tremble, bouncing up and down, and he can't stop it. He leans forward and swallows at the same time so it won't be obvious.

'All I know is what I've told you before—he's looking for Dan's girlfriend. Somehow he thinks you're involved, which is why he came up here.'

'Who's this girlfriend?'

'Some bint called Kelly. Dope-head. Didn't Jimmy tell you?'

'And how did he find out about us being 'apparently' involved? Which as you well know is a bag of shite.'

He swallows again. He wishes he hadn't taken Dan and his dad to Sparkle's shop, now. He was just showing off, wasn't he, as usual. Trying to be helpful. And look where it's got him. He never thought anyone would pick a fight with Sparkle.

'He talked to some tart in Manchester,' he says. 'She must have said something.'

'How do you know?'

'I saw him. I watched him in Manchester.'

Now Pete leans back. He looks over Pedlar John's shoulder. It's Marie with a tray. She sets it down on the low table without looking at either of them.

'Thanks, love,' Pete says, but Marie walks away without saying anything.

'She's pissed off at me again,' Pete says. 'I can't do right for doing wrong these days.'

Pedlar John thinks it's safest to say nothing. He pours himself a cup of tea and takes a slice of lemon cake, which he eats in three bites.

'Jesus,' Pete says. 'Leave the pattern on the plate.'

'Great cake.'

'Marie can cook. About all she can do at the moment. Listen, do you know this tart?'

'I got her name.'

'Good man. And?'

Pedlar John hesitates for a split-second. Pete leans forward again and looks up at him from under his eyelids.

'Don't think about it, Chief. It's not worth the hassle you'd have. And that little pinky you're holding that cup with—you want to keep it, don't you?'

'Sophie. Her name's Sophie. I can find out where she works.'

Pete relaxes. 'You do that. And you can do me another favour, if you like.'

Pedlar John feels good right now. A wave of relief runs through him like a cool breeze. 'I'd like that, Pete.'

'Keep an eye on this Dyke and his pushy little sprog. Anything you think we should be interested in, give us a bell. You've got a number, haven't you?'

'Yes, Pete. Yes, I have.'

'Good. Enjoy your tea. I'm going out. Charlie will take you to the station when you're ready.'

He stands up and reaches into his back pocket, pulling out a roll of twenties. He peels off a handful and throws them on the table. 'That should get you a mortgage on a train ticket home. Watch your step.'

Pedlar John stays seated as Pete leaves the room. His guts are beginning to churn over, and he doesn't think that's down to Marie's lemon cake.

CHAPTER TWENTY-SEVEN

The next morning I drove round to the house Dan shared with Pedlar John. I parked opposite and watched for fifteen minutes but there were no signs of life. It was a nineteen-thirties semi with a stone bay window and a small square of untended garden in front of it. One of the windows had been broken and replaced by a two foot square of plywood. The curtains in the upstairs bedrooms were drawn.

It didn't take much for me to force the door open and slip sideways into the house, exactly as I'd seen them do. Straight ahead of me were stairs that ran beside a tiled passage that went to the back of the house. I went down the passage and found a kitchen piled high with dirty dishes. In a corner a black plastic bag had burst its waste contents onto the linoleum. Through a window I saw a wilderness that would have been an extensive garden if it had been tended properly.

I came back through the house and looked in the two other downstairs rooms. One was being used as a bedroom and stank of unwashed clothing. This looked like Pedlar

John's room, judging by the odd mix of clothing that hung from door handles or was draped over the end of the bed. There were a couple of knitted waistcoats, two pairs of corduroy trousers, a purple velvet jacket and a long trenchcoat that looked like a relic from the German Wehrmacht, circa 1944. I resisted the urge to look through in greater detail because I wasn't sure I would be able to get the smell off my hands.

The other downstairs room was set up as a living room with a small portable TV, an old sofa and a couple of bean bags facing the tiled fireplace. Upstairs there were three small bedrooms and a grimy bathroom. No sign of Pedlar John, though he was apparently still in residence. I couldn't hang around waiting for him and I had no idea where to begin looking for him, so I pulled the front door shut behind me and drove away.

Back in my office, I phoned Trevor Clarke.

'You're like a dog with a bone, aren't you?' he said when he recognised my voice. 'I told you I'd be in touch when I found out anything more.'

'It's not about them,' I said. 'If Jimmy wants to snip the fingers off drug-pushers I'm not going to get in his way.'

'Very noble. So what can I do for you?'

'Tell me what you know about Addison.'

There was a pause at the other end and I imagined Clarke rolling one of his twig-like cigarettes. 'You won't want all the boring stuff,' he said. 'What you'll want to know is that he's got form.'

'What do you mean?'

'I mean he's been nabbed before. About ten years ago, in Derbyshire. He was sacked from a job in the planning office for what was basically insider dealing. Making a profit from land sales. He had a friend, a property developer, who'd buy land and make plans for building houses or whatever on it. He'd get the plans approved—usually with the help of our Mr Addison—then he'd sell the plans on. Of course, Addison had a financial stake in the land as well so he turned a profit. It happened one too many times and someone in the office got wise and shopped him.'

'What happened to him?'

'Slapped wrist, a few hundred pounds fine. He came running back to Halewood with his tail between his legs. Worked his way up again. You'd have thought he'd have kept his nose clean this time around, but some people are too dumb to live. He's going to get found out again.'

'Why Halewood? What's he got going on there?'

'I can tell you that. And you're probably wondering how I know these intimate details of his life.'

'You're a god amongst journalists?'

'Apart from that. It so happens that we ran a 'Day in the Life' feature on him a couple of years ago. You know how it is. A slow news day, who can we get for this exciting news feature? Bingo! A planning officer ... Exciting! He was brought up in Halewood. His dad used to work on the track for Ford, till he died. Young Patrick still sees his mum regularly.'

'Bless,' I said.

CHAPTER TWENTY-EIGHT

It was early afternoon when I arrived in Halewood. The house where Addison's mother lived was neat and looked well-tended. When she answered the door her first thought was to smile at me, which made a nice change from the reactions I'd had from most people in the last week.

'Mrs Addison, my name is Dyke and I'd like to talk to you about your son.'

Her smile widened. 'Oh, are you another one of those fellers from the newspapers? Come on in.'

I didn't like to mislead her, but if it got me the answers I needed without explaining too much then perhaps it wouldn't hurt.

We sat in a small lounge that was a martyr to floral design. She served tea in a delicate china cup on which a single rose bloomed. Then she composed herself and sat opposite me. She was a small woman with thin white hair and fingers so delicate you could almost see through them.

'Patrick's doing very well, isn't he?' she said. 'I told him that he'd do well, if he just stuck to it.'

'Was there a time when he wasn't going to?'

'Well, you know what it's like for a young man. Concentrating can be hard when there are other things to be doing.'

I nodded sagely. I had no idea what she was talking about.

I said, 'You came back here a few years ago, didn't you? Why was that?'

'You've been reading about him,' she said with approval. 'Yes, he really didn't like where he was working before. The people used to get at him because he was so bright, you know. So we talked it over and decided to come back. He's been very successful. Very important job he has.'

'Yes indeed.'

'But then he works so hard, so of course he's successful.'

I was beginning to wonder whether I'd ever get her off this track.

'Mrs Addison, can you tell me anything about the Wilder twins?'

It was as though I'd switched off a light. Her eyes darkened and her face seemed suddenly to be cast in shadow.

'Why are you asking about them?' she said.

'Patrick has dealings with them from time to time. That's right, isn't it?'

'I haven't a clue.'

Her face was closed, her lips a thin line.

'Mrs Addison, you're right. I have been reading about Patrick. I know what he does for a living and I know who he deals with. I don't want to be rude, but I have the impression there's something you're not telling me.'

'I have nothing to say about the Wilder brothers. They're scum.'

'What makes you say that? Do you know them?'

Her eyes turned to the mantelpiece, where a photo of her son stood next to a vase of freesias. He wore his graduation gown, complete with mortar board, and looked very uncomfortable.

She said, 'Patrick grew up with the Wilder boys. They lived the other end of the street. Tearaways even then. Patrick wanted to be good because he wasn't naughty. But they kept bullying him—pushing him and pushing him.'

'What kind of things did they do?'

'Oh, just kids' stuff. Climbing over people's walls. Throwing stones at greenhouses. Firing pellets at dogs.'

'That doesn't sound so bad.'

'It wasn't.' Her eyes came back to me, and now they were tearful. 'But those boys didn't know when to stop. They forced him to steal sweets. Just so they wouldn't beat him up. And of course as they got older it got worse, because they were big boys before they started doing the weightlifting and so on. Patrick didn't stand a chance, poor lad.'

'Did you do anything to stop it?'

She put down her tea cup and folded her hands in her lap.

'His father, God rest his soul, was not a strong man. We complained at the school but no one did anything. It just got Patrick into more trouble.'

I nodded. No one likes a snitch, even when you're eleven years old.

'So what happened?'

'After George died we moved away. There was some insurance money.'

'But then you came back.'

'This was always our home. My family are all local. As I got older, Patrick thought we should come back where I had friends and family. He sees me once a week but I can't expect him to be at my beck and call.'

I looked around again at the home she'd made for herself, full of mementos of other times and other places. Patrick was probably all she had left.

'One more question, Mrs Addison, if I may. Do you know whether Patrick sees the Wilders?'

'Given the way they treated him when they were all boys together, what possible reason would he have to talk to them now?'

CHAPTER TWENTY-NINE

That night I had dinner prepared before Laura arrived home. Chicken casserole with new potatoes boiled in their skins. I'm nothing if not daring in my food preparation.

She sat opposite me and sipped her Chardonnay.

'Have you heard anything about Dan?' she asked. We'd talked about the situation the night before but there was nothing much I could tell her other than that he'd been arrested.

I said, 'I rang Veronica earlier but got voice mail. She hasn't rung back.'

'So shouldn't you be trying the police station or something? The poor lad's probably thinking we've forgotten all about him.'

'I'll only aggravate things if I get involved. Trust me, it's better if Veronica handles it. I'm likely to get him hanged.'

'I can't help thinking we should be doing *something*.'

'I am doing something. What do you think I've been up to all day? Painting my toe-nails?'

'Don't get angry with me, Sam, because things aren't

going the way you planned.'

Her face was neutral, which meant she was either thinking or angry. I was beginning to get a handle on her expressions after several months of close inspection.

I said, 'Just because I'm not jumping up and down, don't think I'm taking this casually.'

'I never said you were.'

'You implied that I haven't done anything to help.'

'Well, that's where you're mistaken. I meant to imply that you haven't done *enough* to help.'

'Glad we cleared that up. Any suggestions?'

'Have you tried to see him?'

'No.'

'Have you talked to the police?'

'No.'

'So what have you done?'

'I've talked to the mother of Patrick Addison, the man who seems to be giving the Wilder twins all their planning permissions.'

She put down her glass and leaned back.

'And this helps how?'

'It seems that they all knew each other when they were kids.'

'So the reasoning is that Addison is helping them out because they're old mates.'

I hesitated. 'That would be the reasoning, except for the fact that they used to bully him. His mother reckons he wouldn't have anything to do with them now because they were always beating him up.'

'But you know different.'

'The evidence is getting more solid.'

She considered this for a moment.

'Okay, so now you're thinking that if Addison is helping

them, it must be because he's still being bullied.'

'That had occurred to me.'

She picked up her drink again and looked at me over the edge of her glass.

'There is another possible scenario.'

'What's that?'

'Addison might be helping them not because they're still bullying him. But because he wants to. Maybe he just turned into a bad man.'

I said, 'He wouldn't be the first.'

CHAPTER THIRTY

I was woken at seven o'clock the next morning by my phone ringing. I mumbled my name into the receiver.

'You're watching Ken Bullard.'

My benefit cheat. I sat up in bed. 'Who's this?'

'He's going to let himself down.' It was a deep masculine voice with a local accent. 'Be at the Town and Country this Saturday.'

The line went dead. As is often the case, it seemed as though someone didn't like Bullard getting away with it. Those petty fights will get you every time.

Dan looked pale and haunted. He sat slumped in his chair without looking directly at either Veronica or me. The interview room was painted a pale grey with a single window placed high on one wall. Our voices echoed off the bare brick-work.

Veronica had told Dan that the police had applied to the magistrate for an extension so that he could be held for further questioning. He didn't take it well.

'Doesn't the fact that I'm up here searching for her tell

those dumb bastards anything?' he said.

'They look for the line of least resistance,' Veronica said. 'You're the closest to a connection they have, so they have to give themselves time to dig up anything relevant.'

'They can look all they want. There's nothing to find.'

'Are you sure?' I said.

'What's that supposed to mean?'

'You lied to me once about her recreational activities. Are you sure you're not lying about anything else?'

'I forgot to mention she's a Russian spy. Is that the kind of thing you mean?'

'Now, boys,' Veronica said. 'You can do this father-son thing on your own time. I'm not wasting my time while you two see who's got the biggest dick.'

Dan smirked, then caught himself and resumed his scowl.

He said to me, 'Have they been to see you yet?'

'I've been out and about. I daresay they'll pull me in soon.'

I didn't think it was worth telling him about my set-to with Inspector Moody by the canal. Moody had seemed to know everything about me that he wanted to, including my relationship to Dan.

'So what am I supposed to do?' he asked. 'I've told them everything I can about her going missing.'

'Did you tell them about the Wilder twins?'

'No. That's still our little secret.'

Veronica turned and looked at me. 'What's this about?'

'Ongoing investigation. Incomplete evidence.'

'Bullshit, Sam. Don't leave Danny boy here in the pokey because you're playing cops and robbers with the bad guys. That's not fair.'

'It's okay,' Dan said. 'I'm his client, so doesn't that give us some privileges?'

Veronica threw up her hands and leaned back in her metal chair.

'Great. Go to it. Leave me out of the loop. Just don't expect miracles when it comes to the courtroom drama.'

I looked at Dan. 'You told me Kelly was American and didn't get on with her parents. What else?'

He shrugged. 'Her dad's some big important tycoon in London. She hardly ever saw him. He was always being whisked about in chauffeur-driven cars.'

'Who did he work for?'

'She didn't say.'

'What's his name?'

'I don't know. Mr Thompson, assuming Kelly gave me her proper name.'

This thought seemed to catch him by surprise. His eyes suddenly became moist and his voice cracked. 'She told me lots of things, but I don't know if they're true, do I? She could have been filling my head with any old crap just to keep me away.'

He brought the back of his hand up to his eyes and rubbed them. Veronica reached out and took his other hand in hers.

Dan said, 'You didn't know her when she was good. She was funny and had lots of energy and lots of friends. She was very optimistic about life.'

I said, 'She had a rich American father. Why wouldn't she be optimistic?'

'You don't understand ... Oh, what's the point. You've got your opinions already. I can see why my mother left you if you're always this open-minded.'

Veronica looked at me sharply, as if warning me not to reply.

But I had no intention of replying. I had nothing to say.

Outside, Veronica told me that she'd keep on top of the situation and let me know when they released him.

'Don't expect to hear anything for a while,' she said. 'I've no doubt the police will want to speak to you so don't give them any grief. They're only doing their job.'

'What I don't understand,' I said, 'is why this suddenly became important.'

'What do you mean?'

'Dan told me that he'd reported Kelly missing weeks ago, in London, and nothing was done. What's happened in the last couple of days to kick this into gear?'

She shrugged. 'There's an escalating timescale to these things. If she didn't turn up after a few days they take it more seriously. Don't try to fathom the mind of the British police, Sam, it'll drive you crazy.'

I knew she was right. Bureaucracy and paperwork were as likely to have an effect on the course of an investigation as anything else. Maybe Kelly's file just floated to the top of the in-tray.

As Veronica said goodbye and walked away, I took Kelly's photograph out of my wallet and looked at it. She was blonde and pretty in that American way with a mouth slightly too full of perfect teeth and a healthy complexion. Heroin can do that for you. I thought about where she was now and what was happening to her. Was she tied up? Imprisoned? Dead? Whatever was happening to her, there was no doubt she was scared, losing any dignity she might have tried to maintain, and probably feeling both helpless and without hope. I couldn't let that situation continue.

And there was one other person I could talk to who might have more information.

CHAPTER THIRTY-ONE

The woman behind the counter at the body shop looked at me critically.

'Lot of work there, Mr Dyke. It's an old car. Next time it'll be a write-off.'

'Yes, mum.'

'No need to get particular.'

'Sorry. Old habits.'

She reached behind and took the keys off a hook.

'There's just the excess to pay.'

I handed over my credit card and she ran it through the swipe machine.

At first I didn't recognise the Cavalier. It had been resprayed down one wing and the new glass in the windscreen was cleaner than it had been for five years. But it still drove like a thoroughbred as I pointed it out of Stoke and up the motorway towards Manchester.

More signs of Spring were evident in the city centre. The trees were greener, the air smelled sweeter, the shoppers wore lighter clothing. I parked and strolled around for a while, peering in shop windows and trying not to look like a detective on a big case. Which was easy, because I didn't know what that would look like.

Eventually I was down with the working girls again. Their clothing got even skimpier with the warm weather so it was easy to pick them out. But I stood and watched for an hour before Sophie turned up. She wore thigh boots and a short denim jacket over a white blouse that was almost completely undone down the front. She stepped from the back of a black BMW then turned and spoke through the window to the driver. She didn't seem happy and ended the conversation by raising one finger to the driver and turning her back on him. The BMW waited a moment, then roared off, its body language clearly indicating Irritation.

She didn't recognise me when I approached, and turned on a smile that had nothing behind the eyes. 'You want company, love?'

'Sophie, it's me. We spoke the other night.'

A frown pinched her features together, then she remembered and released the tension in her body.

'Oh yeah. Thought I recognised you. What you want this time? Collecting on that twenty?'

'Nothing like that. I'm still looking for Kelly and I thought you could help.'

'How? I told you everything I know. Give you her card, dint I?'

I looked at the people dividing around us. I said, 'Let me buy you a coffee.'

'Cost you another twenty. Fifteen minutes.'

'I'll drink quickly.'

She nodded and turned away, heading towards a Costa Coffee a hundred yards down the road.

Once inside she demanded we sit at the back so she could look on to the street. I bought two lattes and she picked out a doughnut too. Now she'd warmed up to me she took off her denim jacket and I saw how thin she was, her collar-bone visible at the top of her blouse, which she'd buttoned up out of courtesy to the other customers. Her face had softened in the warmth and she began to look almost pretty, despite the purple half-moons under her eyes.

'Who are you, then?' she asked. 'Why you so interested in Kelly?'

'People pay me to find other people.'

'What, like Magnum?'

'Without the sex-appeal.'

She giggled. 'Oh, I dunno.'

Great. Now I was an object of lust for a young whore. I couldn't wait to tell Laura.

I said, 'I phoned the number on her card. The one you gave me.'

'Who was it? Sparkle?'

'An American who said he'd phone me right back if I gave my number.'

She bit a huge chunk out of her doughnut and wiped her lips with a finger.

'Her dad, then,' she said. 'Daft cow. Always going on about how much she hated him. Just like her to give his number. She's a daddy's girl, right?'

'Is she?'

Sophie shrugged. 'Who isn't?'

I suddenly saw past her toughness and I didn't like what was there. She'd had a real life once, with a mother and father and probably brothers and sisters. Maybe a solid family background that fell apart when she found her drug of choice.

I said, 'Aren't you worried about Kelly? About what might have happened to her?'

She looked at me over her coffee cup. 'It's what happens. They come and go. Like bleeding Euston Station out there. No one cares if another tart don't turn up for work. You just think, lucky her. One way or another, she's out.'

'Don't you want to get out?'

Her laugh was high and screeching. 'No, mate, I love it, me. Crawled all over by blokes you'd walk on glass to avoid. Don't be fucking soft. Course I want to get out. But I've got problems, ent I?'

'What about Kelly—did she want to get out?'

'The question, as they say, never came up. We never talked much. Just swapped cards.'

'So you don't know anything else about her?'

'Dint say that, did I?'

'What do you mean?'

Now she looked coy and played with the handle of her coffee cup. 'I've got some of her stuff back at my place.'

'What kind of stuff?'

'I dunno. Carrier bags. She stayed over one night when we did a two-some with some guy. She'd gone the next morning before I was up and she left them. Looks like clothes.'

'Can I see them?'

'Another fifteen minutes. Got a fat wallet, have you?'

I drove her round to her flat, but she wouldn't let me in.

'You stay out here,' she said. 'Can't have the neighbours talking, can we?'

She turned and ran up the steps, then through the glass doors of the converted warehouse. Three floors, fifteen flats per floor. Someone was turning a fat profit on rent.

I put Jim White in the CD player. I'd rescued it from the house collection. Third album, getting more subtly musical but still weird. I leaned back but kept my eyes open.

Fifteen minutes later I saw a black BMW turn the corner at the far end of the apartment block and drive away. I waited another five minutes, trying not to think too much, then climbed out of the car and ran up the steps myself, exactly as Sophie had done nearly twenty minutes earlier.

This wasn't America. There was no live-in super to interrogate, no concierge to slip a few quid to. I ran down the first corridor I saw, shouting her name and banging on a couple of doors. No one answered and no one came to see what the fuss was about. I sprinted back to the foyer and ran up the stairs to the next level, running and shouting and banging all over again. It was like an abandoned hotel, no one home.

I found her on the third level. Hers was the only door open. She was lying face up on the floor, both her arms flung outwards, as though she'd been attacked and then left to drop backwards, her arms helpless to prevent her fall. Her face was bloated and slightly blue, as though she'd been trying to hold her breath. She had been almost pretty in life. Death had taken even that from her.

I walked round the flat and looked at everything I could without actually touching. There was no sign of any carrier bags. No sign of much of anything, except some underwear, make-up, drug gear and a radio.

There was a telephone because it was a vital tool of the trade. I took out my handkerchief, picked it up and keyed 999.

CHAPTER THIRTY-TWO

My favourite part of my job—the police interview.

It was a young D.I. who the higher-ups must have thought could handle the murder of a working girl. His name was Boston. He was polite, thorough, and clearly disturbed by the brutality of Sophie's murder. He was also slightly pompous.

'So you were outside for how long?'

'No more than twenty minutes. Track five.'

'What?'

'I put on a CD when she got out the car. It had reached track five according to the display.'

He looked at me closely and made another note.

'And you saw a black BMW turn out of the corner just a few minutes before.'

'I didn't get the license but I think it was her pimp. I saw her get out of the same car an hour before. She and the driver had an argument and the car drove off. It was very irritated.'

'What was?' he asked.

'The car. If you look hard enough you can tell what a car's

thinking.'

'I see. And this one was irritated.'

'I'd almost say angry, but that would be interpreting too much, don't you think?'

He lowered his note-book and looked at his sergeant, who had been standing next to his boss and enjoying himself. I wondered why I was still here, standing in the corridor outside the flat, and hadn't been taken to an incident room elsewhere. Boston must have guessed what I was thinking.

'You're only here because I've been asked to hold on to you,' he said. 'I'll want to talk to you again so don't take your annual holiday to Torremolinos this week, all right?'

'Marbella, actually.'

He walked off to talk to the forensic staff who had started to arrive. Watched by a uniform, I walked to the end of the corridor and looked out of the window. It had begun to rain. The warm weather was on its way out already.

As I watched, a large black saloon pulled up behind the row of police vehicles parked outside the apartment block. Two men in overcoats climbed out and one of them showed some form of ID to the young officer who approached. He stepped back and the two men came up the steps.

A minute later they appeared at the end of the corridor. They both had short hair and wore dark suits and ties beneath their raincoats. Boston saw them and walked over, and the three of them stood talking quietly and occasionally looking over at me. I was certainly a hot date today.

Finally Boston waved me over.

'I'd like you to go with these gentlemen, please.'

'Why?'

'They'd like to ask you some questions.'

'This is a police investigation, isn't it? Straightforward case of strangulation.'

'Correct.'

I hate people who say 'correct' in that formal way that implies at last you've caught up with their advanced thinking.

'So what have these monkeys got to do with anything?' I turned to the closer of the two men, who had a slight grin on his freckled face. 'Who are you? SOCA? Terrorist Prevention? The Gay Police Association?'

His smile faded. 'Come with us and you'll find out soon enough.'

What he said wasn't particularly interesting, but the fact that he said it with an American accent certainly was.

CHAPTER THIRTY-THREE

The rear door of the black saloon opened before we reached it. Freckles guided me towards the back seat and I climbed in. A man with short black hair greying at the sides was watching me without expression. He wore a dark tie and suit, like his henchmen, but his was obviously more expensive. His cuffs extended beyond his sleeves and showed chunky gold cuff-links with a sapphire motif. The cabin smelled of an expensive after-shave lotion and highly-polished shoes. This man was a player.

'Mr Dyke, thanks for coming.'

An American accent.

'The Intelligence community wants to thank you for your help in this matter.' *Madder*.

'What the hell has the Intelligence community got to do with the murder of a prostitute in the back streets of Manchester?'

He pursed his lips.

'I can see where that would appear confusing. It's a question of connections, I guess. This is connected to that, and so forth.'

'If you're trying to clarify things, you're not succeeding.'

He drew a breath and shifted his position on the back seat.

'No, I haven't made myself clear, have I? Your son, Daniel, is being held on suspicion of ... Well, we're not sure, are we? No body has been found. But I think you would be well advised to consider his position.'

I began to feel a pressure in my chest. 'What the hell are you talking about? What's Dan got to do with this—or with you?'

'Let's say we were able to apply a little pressure. To make sure we had your attention.'

I leaned toward him. To his credit, he didn't flinch.

I said, 'If you're telling me you've had Dan arrested so that I would play ball with your spooks, you've seriously overestimated your powers of persuasion.'

His expression, which had remained still, looked briefly pained.

'I'm still not explaining myself well,' he said. 'You have to understand, your son was the only connection we had. We've been looking for Kelly in London. When Dan turned up on the radar in Manchester ... Well, it put another set of gears in motion.'

I turned in my seat and looked back at the apartment block.

'Where does Sophie fit in?'

'Sophie?'

'The dead girl in the flat.'

'Oh, her. I have no idea.'

'Then why are you here?' I said. 'Want some snapshots for your album?'

'We're not here because of her, Mr Dyke.' He allowed

himself a small smile. 'We're here because of you.'

'What does that mean?'

'Our colleagues in the local force were advised that should they come across you, we would welcome the opportunity to, ah, have a chat.'

'So I phone in Sophie's murder and you turn up. Isn't that just a fancy kind of ambulance chasing?'

He pursed his lips again. He was a great purser.

'I think you're missing the point, Mr Dyke. We—that is, I—just wanted to talk to you, face to face.'

'I'm in the phone book. You could have made an appointment.'

He ignored this. 'I wanted to thank you for your help. And to offer you our support.'

'In what?'

He gave me a smile that looked painful. 'In finding Kelly, of course.'

I reached for the door handle but he laid a hand on my arm.

'Please,' he said. 'Perhaps I should introduce myself. My name's Brad Thompson. I'm Kelly's father.'

He told me that while Kelly knew he worked for the US Government, she thought he was a diplomat of some kind, not someone who worked in Intelligence. That explained why they moved around so much when she was growing up.

'The problem is, Mr Dyke, a lot of movement in the domestic arena is not a good environment for someone like Kelly. She's ... Sensitive. She needed more stability than her mother and I realised. When we did, it was too late. I called in a few favours and got myself posted to London in the hope that a new, exciting city where they at least spoke

English would help her get her bearings.'

'Instead she took off.'

He turned away and rubbed at a mark on the car's window.

'She lasted nine months, which I guess is pretty good by her standards. I couldn't watch her every hour of every day, though Lord knows I tried.'

'What about her mother?'

'Yes, what about her ... ' he said, his voice trailing away. His public face was beginning to crack now that we were talking about his daughter.

I said, 'You're what—CIA? With all those resources you still can't find her?'

'I told you, we were looking in the wrong place. When she was seeing your son we knew where she was. I could have brought her back in, but I thought, what was the point? Then she vanished. The first we knew was when Daniel reported it to the police. We've focused all our efforts in London because we didn't think she knew anyone outside of the place.'

'Maybe she's more resourceful than you give her credit for.'

He turned weary eyes on me. 'When your daughter's a drug addict, Mr Dyke, you come to understand the full meaning of the word "resourceful".'

'So what's our next move?'

'I was rather hoping you could tell me.'

'I'm not telling you anything until Dan's released from custody.'

'I'm afraid that's up to your boys in blue. They have to be satisfied that Dan has no connection to Kelly's disappearance.'

'A word from you could help,' I said. 'If the Special

Relationship is still warm and cuddly.'

'Maybe. I'll see what I can do. I'm sorry for using him to get to you, but what else could I do?'

'You could have picked up the phone,' I said, and climbed out of the car.

He reached over and held open the door before I could close it. He held a business card in his hand.

'Here, take this. If you find out anything about Kelly.'

I hesitated.

He said, 'Please.'

I leaned down and took it from him. 'No promises,' I said.

'Of course. Thank you.'

Freckles had come round from the other side of the car, where he'd been smoking and talking on a mobile phone. He shut the door and gave me a nod, then climbed in the driver's seat. The car moved off so quietly I hadn't even heard its engine start.

I walked back to the block of flats and told the uniform on duty that I wanted to talk to D.I. Boston. I explained that I was the person who called in the body and after a brief conversation over his walkie-talkie, he let me in.

'Thought you were off with the big boys,' Boston said. 'Thought you were away to Grosvenor Square to meet James Bond.'

'No, I thought I could give you a hand here.'

He shook his head. 'You people,' he said. 'Always one step ahead of the village bobby, aren't you?'

'Hard not to be without going backwards.'

I took him to one side and told him what I knew about Sophie, Kelly and the Ginger Twins. I told him that a man called Sparkle may have been involved, that he might have had Sophie killed so that she didn't pass any information about Kelly to me.

'But why kill her?' he said. 'These girls can be scared off if you look at them the wrong way. They don't want anything coming between them and their supply. A bit of a slapping and some harsh words and she would have sworn blind she'd never heard of whatshername, Kelly.'

'If it was Sparkle,' I said. 'He did it because he was scared. I've seen him up close and he's easily scared. And he's too dumb to do anything but lash out. Track him down and he'll lead you straight up the chain.'

'What, to these twins?'

'Yes. Or my name's not James Bond.'

CHAPTER THIRTY-FOUR

It wasn't going to be easy. She knew that. He was a big man and nothing seemed to hurt him. Maybe it was the steroids. Maybe that was a side-effect—it deadened all your feeling, made you invulnerable. It didn't matter. She wasn't going to fight with him, anyway.

She'd been working on the plan for about a week now. She'd studied him each time he came down the folding steps—the way he reached the bottom rung, leaned over to the left while holding on with his right hand, then dropped off the steps as if he was trying to show how dainty he was. It was all part of his act, his 'look-at-me' routine that was intended to make him appear light and 'normal,' not like the lumbering beast he actually was.

He usually had clothes or food under one arm, so he was especially careful not to seem clumsy. But she wanted him to come down without anything in his hands, this time. She wanted him to be confident.

And it had to be early evening, when she was sure he was there. When he delivered stuff it was usually first thing in the morning. She didn't know why. She thought perhaps he wanted to deal with her before his gang arrived. She'd heard them up there, talking, so she knew they turned up most mornings. Then they'd either go out and beat up some people, or hang around in the house, clumping around with their heavy boots overhead. Then most nights about seven o'clock, he'd lift the trapdoor and look down at her. He wouldn't lower the stairs, just poke his head in and ask whether she was all right, whether she needed anything. She always said no, just to get rid of him. But he was pretty regular so she assumed it was part of his Neanderthal routine — come home, eat food, check hostage, watch TV, go to bed. *Duh.*

The final part of the plan occurred to her when she found the camera lens. It was no more than a quarter of an inch across, concealed in a weird abstract painting he'd hung on the wall. It was some kind of avant-garde shit with lines and circles and swirls, and one day she noticed a glint coming from one of the marks in the canvas. When she got up close she saw that a part of the picture had been carefully cut away and that a lens of some kind was installed behind it.

Good.

Now she had a way of fetching him in when she was ready, not when *he* wanted to come.

She'd been lying on the floor about five minutes when she heard the trap door swing open. She increased her shaking, swinging her head back and forth and moaning more loudly. If she'd been able to foam at the mouth she'd have tried that, too, but he was probably dumb enough to be taken in just by this.

'You all right, girl?' he shouted down. 'What's up?'

She shifted her position to look up at him, then moaned

again and turned away, making her arms and legs tremble. She was beginning to tire but she knew this was her last chance.

The ladder snapped metallically into place and she heard his weight hit the first rung.

'You're not well, are you, Princess?' he said. 'All those crap meals you eat. You should cook proper. I'll get you some real veggies and you can learn how to peel a spud.'

He'd reached the last rung. From her position on the floor she saw him hang on to the lower half of the ladder with his right hand and prepare to drop off.

As he did, she rolled over towards him. For some reason her father knew martial arts and had taught her how to snap-kick, and she hooked one foot around the back of Jimmy's leg, then kicked out at his knee. She'd hoped to hear a crack or for him to shout out in pain, but he didn't. He merely said, 'Ow!' and fell backwards, behind the ladder, his head striking the corner of her bed.

She got to her feet instantly and leaped upwards on to the ladder. From the corner of her eye she saw Jimmy begin to rise. There was a moment's eye contact between them, then she was up the ladder like a sprite and folding the trap door down. She thought there might be a bolt or something to hold it down, but there was only a key pad. She pressed a few keys then ran.

She sprinted from the room and ran up half a dozen steps, into the foyer. It was still light outside and she could see Jimmy's red Corvette through the windows either side of the front door.

She ran to the door and turned the handle—but the door wouldn't open. She tried again, searching for catches or bolts that might be holding the door closed. There was nothing

She took a step back and looked around. There were

doors to a kitchen and a lounge—perhaps there'd be a rear exit. She ran through the kitchen to the back door and tried it. Locked again. She pounded at the wood and pulled again but it made no difference. It wouldn't move. She felt her eyes growing wet as her panic rose.

She ran out into the hallway and through into the lounge. Patio windows at the end of the room, but she knew immediately it would be hopeless. They were made the same as the ones in the kitchen. She turned the handle but it made no difference—nothing opened.

She stepped back and screamed, a howl of frustration and pain that frightened her. And time was moving on. He could be battering his way out of the room by now.

Looking around, she saw a dining table and chairs. With a strength she didn't know she had, she picked up one of the chairs and threw it at the patio windows. It bounced off and fell to the tiles, where a leg snapped.

She turned again, looking for something else ... And saw Little Jimmy in the doorway, a big smile on his dumb potato face.

'Need this, Princess?' he said, lifting a small electronic device that looked like a TV remote control. He stepped into the room. 'Never go anywhere without it, me.'

She backed away from him, her heart pounding.

'I built this place,' he said. 'You didn't think I wouldn't put in a couple of extras, did you? State of the art, Princess. All mod cons. I like me gadgets. Everything controlled from one handy zapper.'

He raised it towards her and made as if to press a button. She flinched as though a cage might drop from the roof.

'Don't worry,' he said. 'I'm not going to punish you. Shows you're getting stronger, which is good. Now let's go back downstairs and make you all cosy again.'

She raised her arms as he stood close to her, intending to push her fingers in his eyes—another trick from her father. But as he came closer, all her energy drained and her shoulders slumped.

'That's right,' he said. 'I'll take you back there. Don't worry about it.'

He bent and picked her up. He carried her back through the hall and to the trap door, which he'd obviously opened from inside. She closed her eyes and tried not to take in the dead smell of his body as he carried her down into the cell. He stood her upright, holding her shoulders as though she might collapse.

'Get something to eat,' he said. 'I'll look in again in the morning.'

Just before he climbed up the ladder he turned and took a wrap from his pocket, throwing it on the bed next to her. Kelly stared at it, fighting an impulse she knew she couldn't resist. She felt Jimmy watching her and lifted her eyes defiantly to his. He shrugged and gripped the ladder to start his ascent. Before he had climbed the first rung, Kelly had closed her hand over the silver packet.

She looked forward to the oblivion.

CHAPTER THIRTY-FIVE

I have few visitors, so when there was a knock on my door I took a moment to look through the curtains before opening it. Pedlar John stood on my doorstep, looking down at his feet and mumbling to himself. He wore a long green anorak, torn jeans and his usual woollen hat—standard eco-warrior uniform.

When I opened the door he looked up at me but didn't say anything. He raised a hand in a kind of 'how's it going, dude' salute, then put that hand and its partner into his coat pockets.

'I give to charity through a direct debit,' I said. 'What do you want?'

'Don't give me shit, Mr Dyke,' he said. 'Please.'

At least he wasn't calling me Dad. I opened the door wider.

'Do you want to come in?'

'Nah, that's all right. I'd only get your place dirty. Look at me—you'd think I slept in the park, wouldn't you? If you saw me in the street, like.'

'Have you been back to your place?' I asked.

'Why? What's happened?'

Now I was getting exasperated. 'The police have taken Dan into custody.'

'That's wack. He's had nothing to do with it.'

'What do you mean?'

'Stands to reason. She was seen up here after Dan reported her missing. Why would he do that if he knew she was still around?'

I stared at him.

'Why do I always get the impression you know more about all this than you let on?'

He shuffled from side to side.

He said, 'I don't always know what I know, all right? Someone says something and bang, I get the picture. I meet a lot of people, Mr Dyke. I don't always remember who said what and when. Too many mushrooms.'

He gave me a dirty-toothed grin.

I said, 'You came here for a reason, didn't you?'

'I guess I did. I'm not good at this kind of stuff.'

'What kind of stuff? What's going on?'

He seemed to remember something. 'Hey, the police picked me up. Well I think he was the police. Big guys with short hair and muscles. Took me to the canal and stuck me in a room.'

Moody, the Inspector from the special unit, or whatever they were.

'What did you tell them?'

He grinned. 'Whatever the hell they wanted to know. Not arguing with those fuckers, no way.' He saw how I was looking at him. 'They had you too, didn't they? They work you over? Bet they tried, you being Mr Big Private Detective and all. I bet they just love you.'

'Whatever Moody advised you to do, I recommend you do it.'

He turned sullen again. 'Yeah. Bastards. My arm still hurts where they grabbed me.'

'John, I've got to —'

'You need to watch out, Mr Dyke,' he blurted. 'Things are happening.'

'You'd better think about what you're saying, John.'

'I know, I know.' He seemed disgusted with something — maybe himself. 'It's like Peter and the Wolf, ain't it? No, not that — the boy who cried wolf. That's it. I've said stuff to you before, haven't I? Like warnings and so on.'

I stepped forward. 'Listen, you wart, say what you've got to say and then get lost. I don't want you around here. Or around Dan.'

'I'm just saying ... '

'What? What minuscule thought is crossing from one side of your tiny brain to the other?'

'Just that things are happening —'

'You're repeating yourself.'

'So now would be a good time to do something.'

I went to close the door but he stuck out a hand to stop me.

'You don't like me, Mr Dyke. But I like Dan. And you can't tell me I'm lying.'

He took his hand from the door and walked away. I wanted to bring him back and stretch him over hot coals, but I realised that would get me nowhere. With a brain as fried as his was, there was little hope of eliciting any truth. I closed the door and went back inside.

Sitting at the kitchen table with a cup of coffee I thought over the conversation, but still made no sense of it. He'd obviously wanted to tell me something but either couldn't remember what it was, or was too anxious to make himself plain.

The only clear message he seemed to transmit was that things were coming to a head. But what things? What did he know? What could he possibly know? When I met him in Manchester I thought he'd been following me. But maybe he was on some other mission. Perhaps he was meeting someone, arranging something, organising some kind of event that was related to Kelly and Dan and their predicament.

From the beginning I hadn't liked Pedlar John. I'd thought he was shifty, cunning and out for his own benefit. I couldn't believe he'd turned good Samaritan for no good reason, but he did seem to want to warn me ... Although what he was warning me about, neither of us was clear.

My thoughts kept coming back to Jimmy and Pete Wilder and their relationship with Addison, the planning officer. There was no doubt in my mind they were connected to each other. And I had a growing conviction the Wilders were connected in some way to Kelly's disappearance. If it had been Sparkle leaving Sophie's flat, and leaving her dead on its floor, then her death was linked to the Wilders. I wasn't even sure that Sparkle had it in him to kill Sophie. Which meant that he might have been chauffeuring someone else. Maybe one of the Wilders. If that were true, and she was murdered because of her link to me or to Kelly, then I had to push them further. To do that, I had to get inside Little Jimmy's house and have a look around. I couldn't do that by myself.

But I knew someone who could help.

Saturday night at the Town Country was line dance time. I had to park on the road and squeeze my way through the crush at the bar to get a view of the dance floor. There was a lot of denim and men wearing leather waist-coats. Fiddle music bounced off the walls, nearly drowning the voice of the caller, who stood on a little dais looking very pleased with himself.

I'd seen Ken Bullard with his wife, so I knew that the woman he was dancing with wasn't her. She was younger, slimmer, and had blonder hair. Ken had moved up-market, dodgy leg or no.

I sat and watched for a while, taking a seat near the floor. In a break, I saw Ken's partner talking to another woman. She had big hair and a tee-shirt that read, 'Ride it Cowboy'. When Ken's partner moved away, I found the opportunity to put myself next to the woman with the tee-shirt, though I wasn't inclined to take her up on the offer.

'Isn't that Marjorie?' I said, leaning over with my best friendly smile.

The woman, who was in her forties and obviously enjoying the music and excitement, followed my gaze to Ken's partner. 'No, that's Alice. Do you know her?'

'I thought I knew her husband.'

We were talking quite loudly against the music.

'Well that's not her husband, if that's what you're thinking,' she said. 'She got divorced last year. I don't know this new feller. Good dancer, though.'

'Yes, he is, isn't he?' I said. 'What happened to her husband then?'

She turned to me. 'You're nosy. What's it to you?'

I held up my hands. 'Sorry, it's because I thought I knew her. From school.'

She accepted this. 'It was bad,' she said. 'He was jealous. Wouldn't let her out. Wouldn't go with her anywhere. She had to set the police on him once the divorce was over. He kept turning up, watching her, like.'

I nodded. At least I knew who owned the male voice that had woken me with the early telephone call, telling me to be at the Town and Country in the first place. Now I had the evidence that would put Ken Bullard in trouble, making at least one other person happy: Alice's ex-husband.

It always amazed me how spiteful people could get when they were frustrated. I'd seen people do really bad things when their spite made them ignore the consequences of their actions. I expected to see it happen again.

CHAPTER THIRTY-SIX

The third was even easier than the first two had been. It was almost as though they wanted to be punished for what they did. They'd walk up to him with their eyes turned downwards or to one side, then ask a simple question: 'You want something?'

He'd look at them and feel a surge of power through his chest and arms. Yes, he wanted something. He wanted to push the little turd back into the alley he'd crawled out of and smash his face with a brick.

But he didn't. Not just then. Instead he'd lift his chin slightly, as if to say, 'Where we going to do it?', then follow the dealer into a less public place.

He always went through with the transaction first. Never haggled. Just asked how much then took out his wallet. They were always nervous, probably because of his size, and they constantly looked left and right to check out whether any problems were about to walk in. Hand over the cash. Take the wrap. Then he'd relax, put his hands in his pockets, grip the snippers in his curled fingers. He guessed most buyers would want to get away in a hurry, so the dealers were always worried when he hung around. They must have wondered what he was after, why he wanted to stand there, shooting the breeze.

The third one had collapsed as soon as he saw the snippers. He must have read about the first two and knew what was coming. He was a scrawny kid in his twenties with long hair that was so greasy it looked wet. Jimmy didn't actually like touching him. But he forced himself to grab the man's right hand while leaning into him with the bulk of his body. The man was now pressed up tight against a brick wall, the side of a house that looked abandoned.

Jimmy spread the man's fingers. Behind his back he heard crying and whimpering and thought he smelled shit—the dirty bastard had shit himself, he was so afraid.

'You shouldn't have done that,' Jimmy said. 'I was only going to take your little finger. Now I'm going to move one up.'

The man had wailed again, but Jimmy shut him up with one quick squeeze of his secateurs. Then he had to lower him to the ground, because he'd fainted. Jimmy took out some gauze and cotton wool from his pocket and wrapped it around the man's stump. Then he looked around until he found the finger and placed it inside a glassine bag, which he dropped inside his pocket.

That had been two days ago. In between he'd sorted out that tart Sophie and had dealt with Kelly's laughable attempt to escape. Sophie should have kept her mouth shut. Pedlar John had done well to find out that she'd spoken to Dyke, and then tell Pete about it. But she'd been stupid. She was just asking for trouble, so he gave it to her. He hadn't really intended to kill her, though. Waste of good income. Didn't know his own strength sometimes. It was a pity he didn't have his snippers with him, too. It would have been good to have a couple of trophies.

There was a lot going on in his life at the moment, and he didn't like it. He preferred it when he was dealing with one thing at a time. Bringing the stuff in from Africa was enough to handle at the moment. He could do without Kelly and that investigator and all this business with Addison getting cold feet. He could feel the tension in his chest and neck. He'd worked out today, and that helped, but it only needed a conversation with Pete for it all to come back to the surface again, like heartburn.

The Hulme arch was visible from where he was standing. They'd cleaned up the area and put in a big steel arch like one half of a mcdonalds sign, but he'd been told where to go if he wanted a deal.

He'd parked the Corvette half a mile away and walked down here. Got looks from some of the hard boys who walked past him, rolling their shoulders as if they were American pimps. They'd all watched Eminem and those black guys on MTM, holding their guns sideways and making their stupid E and W signs with their fingers. Teenagers today—stupidest lot of brainless twats. No sense of pride in themselves, copying everything from other people instead of making it up themselves. When him and Pete had been young they used to wag off school and go down the canal. Get some fresh air, ride their bikes, kick a ball. None of this standing round on corners texting each other. They hadn't exactly been masterminds, but at least they knew what they wanted.

A voice said, 'You looking for something?'

A woman who was probably in her thirties, short dark hair, bright red lips. Not a tart—not dressed for it.

'What you got?' he asked.

'What do you think? Liquorice Allsorts?'

'Lemme see.'

She stepped away from him and he followed her. The houses were thirties terraces, big redbricks with concrete bay windows, probably rented by students. She crossed a road and they were in a park, empty now night had come. The park was full of trees and bushes, and there were lots of places that gave cover. Jimmy looked around and got himself ready.

The woman opened a large handbag and brought out a couple of silver wraps. 'Good stuff,' she said. 'Afghanistan's finest.'

Jimmy grinned. 'How much?'

She told him, and he took out his wallet. 'Go buy another kilo,' he said, handing over the notes.

While she counted it, he reached into his pocket and pulled out his snippers. She must have seen something or felt something because her head came up quickly and she looked at his face.

'Shit,' she said, 'You're him. Fuck off away from me.'

She was fumbling in her bag and Jimmy realised she was probably reaching for a knife or a spray. He almost laughed – the pushers were tooling up now they knew someone was after them. He reached out and snatched the bag from her, then threw it away. She turned but he caught her and pulled her back. She opened her mouth to scream but Jimmy's hand was too quick.

He pulled her into the shade of a large bush. She wriggled fiercely in his arms, and then suddenly went limp. Jimmy laid her on the ground. Her eyes were closed — she'd fainted.

He stood over her for a moment, then reached in again for his snippers. He pulled them out of his pocket and knelt down on the grass next to her. He could smell the damp earth of a flower bed a few feet away and heard voices from the other end of the park.

He thought afterwards that he must have been distracted, because he never saw her hand come up at him, holding a rock that she grabbed from the flower-bed. It cracked him on the temple and he couldn't help himself, he went over. She was quick enough to get to her feet and she must have thought she'd got away.

But despite his size Jimmy was light on his feet. All that skipping in the gym, he told himself, as his arm went out and hooked her foot. She fell down with a grunt and he was on her. He didn't bother with his snippers now. He raised his fist and caught the woman flush on her cheekbone, which smashed immediately. Then he started properly.

As he was doing it, he watched himself, as though he was standing ten feet back and was an interested spectator in what he was doing. He knew that the beating he gave the woman wasn't really because of what she'd done to him. He was just letting off steam. All the problems he was dealing with at the moment formed a hard knot in his chest that worked its way out down his arms and into his fists. They became clubs, without feeling and without any real control. He watched himself raise his fists one after the other, then smash them down into the woman's face, her chest, her shoulders. When he'd strangled Sophie he'd left feeling disappointed, because she'd put up no fight at all. Sparkle had to drag him away, he felt so low. And dealing with Kelly had been like running around after a kid. Not a challenge, really.

Pete was getting on his nerves, too. Always getting at him. Bollocking him for taking the steroids. On his case about the shipment, where was it now, this minute, this second. Up his own arse without any consideration for anyone else. Marie egging him on, standing behind like a wizened witch, cigarette stuck in her mouth and stinking up the house.

So he had this tension building inside him and this woman in the park was just unlucky. It wasn't her fault, but she was going to bear the brunt of his frustration.

Eventually he stood up and walked away. He didn't look back. He didn't want to see. He wasn't proud of what he'd done. It was just something that happened.

He walked back to his car and sat with the motor running for a few minutes. He realised that he was taking shallow breaths so concentrated for a while on breathing deep, taking in the smell of the leather, the odour of the blood congealing on his hands.

He looked around, getting his bearings. He engaged first gear and pointed the car out of Manchester, taking the spur off the M56 and heading South.

Thirty minutes later he was parked outside Sam Dyke's house, watching the shadows move around inside.

CHAPTER THIRTY-SEVEN

My phone rang at 8.30 Monday morning, just as I was leaving the house. It was Veronica.

'Good news, Sam. Your boy becomes a free man again this morning.'

'Watch out, world.'

'Shall I meet you there?'

I said I'd be there and after she hung up I phoned Laura and told her.

'Great,' she said. 'I'll come along too. Make him feel looked after.'

I was distracted as I drove to the station. When I'd got up the day before I found a line of syringes stuck in the ground either side of the driveway. There was nothing to identify where they'd come from—but there didn't need to be. Only the Wilder twins would have the nerve to make a point like that.

I'd thought about telling Laura when I spoke to her later that day, but decided against it. Part of her was already mad with me for still being involved with the Wilders, even though I believed they were connected to Kelly's disappearance. If I'd told her about this I thought her brains might bubble out of her ears.

Laura and Veronica were standing outside the station, talking, when I arrived.

'Have you seen him?' I asked Veronica.

'They're just unadmitting him,' she said. She didn't seem to be her usual self.

'What's up?' I asked. I looked at Laura but she shrugged.

Veronica said, 'Spending time in the clink isn't fun. Don't expect him to be full of sweetness and light.'

'Great,' said Laura. 'Two miserable so-and-sos at home. I'm looking forward to this.'

'Your problem,' I said, 'is that you don't know when you're well off.'

'Puh-lease ... '

We turned at that moment as the glass doors opened and Dan came out. He looked pale and tired around the eyes. Laura went to him and gave him a hug while Veronica waved at him. He looked at me.

'Any luck with Kelly?' he asked.

'Fine thanks, how are you?'

He shook his head and looked away. 'Can we go somewhere else?' he asked. 'I don't like hanging around here.'

Veronica said her farewells and zoomed off with her usual briskness.

'Why don't you come with me,' Laura said to Dan, giving me the eye and leading him by the elbow towards her Saab soft-top. 'See you back at the house,' she said to me over her shoulder.

I stood for a moment, looking after them and feeling like the wallflower who nobody wants to know or even take to the party.

By the time I got back to the house Laura had put the kettle on and Dan was upstairs, changing his clothes.

Laura looked at me and pursed her lips. 'Be nice,' she said. 'He's quite angry about what's happened to him.'

'Does he blame me for it?'

'Not directly.'

'Then what does he want from me?'

She came and laid her hands on my chest, looking up at me with half a smile. 'I don't think he knows it, but he wants a dad.'

'I don't remember volunteering. I feel like an understudy thrown on stage without a rehearsal.'

'I think you're a natural. Just treat him like a grown up and show an interest. I know — you could act like a detective. That would be a novelty.'

My smart reply was on its way when Dan appeared in the kitchen door. He'd changed into the upmarket trousers and shirt that he'd bought for work. He must have seen the question on my face.

'Laura says I should go back to work as soon as possible.'

'Good idea,' I said. 'Don't let the bastards grind you down.'

Laura poured tea and we all sat at the breakfast table like a stage family who didn't actually know each other very well.

'I haven't told anyone at work,' Laura said. 'They don't need to know. There's been nothing on the news about Kelly or Dan's arrest so there's no need to get them all excited.'

'I've got to practise my cough,' Dan said. 'Pretend I've been ill.'

I looked at them both.

'You've got this all worked out, haven't you?'

'Well someone's got to do *some*thing,' Dan said.

'What's that supposed to mean?'

'Kelly's still missing. You're no further on. Let's just say I'm glad I'm not paying you.'

Laura stood up. 'Boys! Pack it in. Now.'

'But— '

'I don't want to hear another word. Dan, finish your tea. I'll take you into work. Sam, get back to doing whatever you were doing. We'll see you later tonight.'

Dan finished his tea and fetched his jacket from the cupboard under the stairs. Laura looked at me with a warning in her eyes and picked up her handbag and car keys. For the second time in less than an hour I watched them leave together. I began to wonder whose son Dan was, exactly.

CHAPTER THIRTY-EIGHT

I went back to my office in case something exciting was happening there.

No dice. So I went down to the kitchen I shared with the shop assistants from the furniture store and made myself an instant coffee. I spent five minutes talking to a man I knew slightly who'd worked there for more than fifteen years, before Tommo had come on the scene.

'It's a good business,' he said, swigging tea from a cup marked "World's Best Dad". 'People always need furniture. Like your line of work, I expect. There's always people in trouble, eh?'

Yes, I thought, and it's usually me.

'The thing is,' he went on, 'is that as you get older, you see that people are all essentially the same. The same drives, motivation, aspirations. That's what makes it easy to sell to them. We're quite straightforward. We're not complicated animals.'

I thought again about the line of syringes outside my front door. Obviously they were meant as a warning from the Wilder Twins. Another one. They must have realised that trashing my house and car hadn't worked, so they were getting a little more ... Threatening. But why syringes? There had been ten of them, five lined up either side of the path that led to my front door, stuck into the ground like an honour guard. What were they trying to tell me by using drug paraphernalia? Was this in store for me? Would they find me, strap me to Little Jimmy's chair and pump me full of dope, like Gene Hackman in French Connection 2?

Or were they just the first significant symbols they could lay their hands on? Knowing Little Jimmy's predilections, I supposed I should be glad they weren't human fingers, pointing upwards to the Heaven they were likely to hasten me towards.

'Are you all right?' the man—who naturally was called Barry—asked me.

I looked at him. He seemed concerned, as if I were about to drop to the floor and foam at the mouth.

'I'm fine,' I said. 'Just thinking about the insights you're offering me into life's mysteries.'

He was baffled. 'Well, you know. Age has its benefits.'

'And how old are you?'

'Thirty-four next week.'

'My point exactly.'

Back in my office, I spent a couple of hours writing up my report on Ken Bullard. I included the date and the time that I'd witnessed him performing at the Town and Country, swinging his partner, dosie-doe. It's times like those when you have to disengage the human side of your personality. At one level I could empathise with him—he got injured at work so felt he had a right to take it out on someone. On the other hand, he was knowingly depriving the government of money that could have gone elsewhere. I gritted my teeth and wrote the words, then made myself feel better by typing out my invoice for the job. I stuck it all in an envelope and went down the street to post it.

At my desk again, I took out one of the business cards I'd been given in the last few days and looked for the telephone number. I dialled. It rang twice before being picked up.

'Can we meet?' I said.

'Sure. What do you have?'

'I think I need some help.'

'Give me a time and place.'

I told him my address and we arranged to meet at four o'clock.

'I'll be there,' Kelly's father said.

'I'll be waiting,' I replied.

CHAPTER THIRTY-NINE

He came with two men who were different to the ones I'd met outside Sophie's apartment. They were bigger, more alert, more serious. One was called Dexter—'Call me Dex'—and the other was called Dorian. He nodded at me but said nothing.

They came in first and looked around. They noted the smashed TV and the paint marks on the carpet, glancing at each other as if confirming something in my profile. They looked in all the bedrooms and went out to the garage. When they came back in Dexter said, 'Nice set of weights out there. You box?'

'My ballet teacher tells me I need to strengthen my calves.'

Dorian raised his eyebrows at Dexter then went to the door and nodded towards the car in which Brad Thompson sat waiting.

A moment later he appeared in the doorway, taking off his leather gloves. Dorian and Dexter stood back, one by the window looking out, one by the doorway, looking in. Classic positioning. Thompson shook my hand.

'So what's this about?'

'I need to know some things first.'

He raised an eyebrow. 'Shoot.'

'How independent are you?'

'I have a case officer, but she doesn't look over my shoulder.'

'How many men can you get hold of?'

He looked at Dexter and Dorian. 'Eight immediately. Another four in two days.'

'Armed?'

'What's this about, Dyke?'

'Answer the question.'

He found a seat and unbuttoned his coat. 'We can get hold of ordinance if necessary. Though I shouldn't think we'd need it on mainland Britain, would we?'

Dexter snorted. Thompson gave him a sharp look and he went back to searching my front garden for indications of terrorist incursion.

I said, 'Can your men be trusted?'

'For Christ's sake, Dyke! Give us a break here. We may be colonials but we know how to do our job.'

I sat in the chair opposite him. I liked it that he was rattled. I didn't want him to think it was going to be easy to walk in and take over the plan I had in mind.

'Okay,' I said. 'Do you want to find your daughter?'

'If you insult my intelligence once more, me and my untrustworthy guys here are leaving.'

'You have to operate within certain boundaries, don't you?'

He looked at me warily. 'The law of the land applies to all of us.'

'So what if I were to suggest an operation requiring eight

men breaking into a house to perform an illegal search?'

'I'd have to ask why you're coming to me and not using your own law enforcement system.'

This was a good question and one for which I had no real answer. I said nothing and waited to see if Thompson was as bright as I hoped.

I watched him think for a while, then he said, 'It's got nothing to do with legal or illegal, has it? You want to send a message. And you want to use my boys as Western Union.'

'Plus, I can't afford to be seen to be wrong.'

'Can't lose your credibility with the locals,' he said.

'Crying wolf won't help me later on.'

'Whereas I'm out of the loop.' He shifted in his seat and began to do up his coat. 'This is too risky, Dyke. I have credibility issues too. My boss is beginning to ask some less-than-friendly questions about my use of time. Like, why am I spending so much of it in this arctic wasteland?'

'You're a company man, then.'

He stood up and looked down at me. 'Don't give me that horse-shit. This is my daughter you're talking about here. Do you think I give a good goddamn about what my boss thinks?'

'I think you're—what is it you Yanks say?—conflicted. You've got a responsible position, a decent standard of living, an ongoing career that will probably end in Washington rather than Afghanistan. On the other hand, you feel guilty about the way you treated Kelly, the way you've dragged her around the world while you played Spy versus Spy.'

'I didn't —'

'What?'

Thompson hesitated, then looked at Dexter and Dorian and flicked his head. They left their posts and went outside.

Once they were gone and the door was shut, he said, 'It was never my idea to bring Kelly. It was her mother.' He slumped into his seat again. 'Gabrielle wanted to raise Kelly as a "citizen of the world", whatever the hell that meant. I could have taken shorter tours and left them at home. But Gabrielle wanted to be with me. And then when Kelly was born, she wanted her to be with us.'

'It wasn't easy,' I said.

'Damn right. I spent more time worrying about the pair of them than doing my job.'

'And Kelly thought you were too hard on her.'

He looked away, suddenly self-conscious. 'You try to do right by the people you love. And they don't get it. They just don't get it.'

I was quiet for a moment, leaving him with his thoughts. Then I said, 'Six men, plus you and me, tomorrow night. Can you do it?'

He turned back to me and leaned forward in the chair. 'Let's hear what you've got.'

Thompson and his men had been gone about five minutes when my phone rang. It was Dan.

'Oh, you're there,' he said. 'I tried your office and your mobile's switched off.'

'Sorry, I didn't know I was supposed to report in.'

'Don't start. I was just wondering if there's any news.'

'When I hear, you hear.'

There was a pause and I heard the noise of loud conversation behind him, as if he were in a pub or cafe. Dan said, 'So are you actually doing anything? I mean right now?'

'Just sitting here waiting for your call.'

'That's what I thought.'

The tone in his voice suddenly got to me. He'd gone past angry and was now in despondent. As a result, I said something I shouldn't have.

'If it makes you happy, I've arranged for something to happen.'

'What do you mean?' His voice picked up a little excitement.

'I'm not going into detail because you'll only want to get involved, and I promise you now, that's not going to happen.'

'All right, all right. But give me a hint.'

'Let's just say Little Jimmy is in for a surprise.'

CHAPTER FORTY

He watches Dan close his phone. Looking happy, now. He was miserable as bollocks five minutes ago, now he's fizzing.

'Good news, mate?' he says, trying to sound casual.

'Wouldn't you like to know?' Dan says, cocky, lifting his pint and smiling with his eyes over the top of the glass.

This isn't a good development. Something's going on between Dan and his dad. Pedlar John looks round the pub, searching for an idea, something to go with.

'So tell me,' Dan says, interrupting his train of thought. 'Where'd you get to?'

'Me, mate? Nowhere. Here and there. Out and about.'

'Slippy bugger, aren't you?'

'I don't know what you mean,' he says, pretending to be offended. 'If you must know, I'm getting out of that place.'

'What—our place?'

He nods. 'Don't like the area. Too much riff-raff. What you laughing at?'

Dan has nearly spilled his drink. Puts it carefully down on a mat and wipes his mouth with the back of a hand.

'You certainly fancy yourself,' Dan says. 'I'll give you that. Never short on confidence.'

'If you don't stick up for yourself, nobody else will. My dad told me that.'

Dan nods. 'Dads do that, don't they? Tell you stuff. Then it's your job to ignore it.'

John raises his pint. 'I'll drink to that, me.'

'So tell me, where is it your family's from?'

He feels himself beginning to sweat and puts his hands under the table to hide them.

'Yorkshire,' he says. 'Big place, over there on the right.'

'Whereabouts, exactly? You've never said. I might have "roots" there myself, me coming from Yorkshire stock and all.'

'Oh, a small place. You won't have heard of it. One of those mining villages. Slag heaps. Miners with funny hats on, carrying canaries.' He attempts a laugh but his throat is too dry.

'It's just that you don't sound Yorkshire. Haven't got the accent, know what I mean?'

'Social mobility,' John says proudly, repeating something he'd heard someone say on television. 'We moved out when I were a nipper.'

He can't get past the idea that Dan is pushing him. He's smiling, but he keeps asking questions. He's never done that before. It makes him feel uncomfortable. Every conversation he has these days makes him feel uncomfortable. It's beginning to piss him off.

Dan's still going at it. 'But you've got family there?'

'No, not really —' He catches himself. 'Well, uncles and aunts. Not immediate—mum and dad, like.'

'So where *were* you brought up?'

'Oh, we moved around. Spent some time up here, a

couple of years down south.'

'Your dad, was it?'

'Yeah, yeah. His job moved him around.'

He wants to get off this subject now. He's reached the limit of his ability to invent. In fact he'd never known his dad and he'd run away from his mum when she got her tenth boyfriend in two years. He knew at first sight he was in for a beating or two, so he split, lived on the streets in Brighton before moving up to Liverpool. That's when he'd first bumped into the Twins. Then he'd moved to Crewe when it got too hot for him to stay.

He watches as Dan finishes his pint. He has an idea.

'Want another?' he asks.

Dan looks at his watch then shrugs. 'Okay. Same again.'

He goes to the bar and orders a pint and a double vodka. When they arrive he looks round swiftly then tips the vodka into the beer and stirs it. Gets a Coke for himself.

Back at the table he gets Dan talking about Kelly, anything so long as he's not asking questions.

'So have you got plans if you find her?' he asks.

Dan looks at him through hooded eyes. 'There's no "if" about it,' he says, taking another swig from his drink. 'We're getting closer.'

'That's good then. How's that working, exactly?'

Dan taps the side of his nose — never you mind.

'Something's happening, right? You were talking to your dad and he told you something, didn't he? You can't fool me, mate.'

'Why would I want to do that? Why should I want to fool the great fooler?' He laughs right in Pedlar John's face. Really pissing him off, now.

'I've done my best by you,' he says. 'I tried to help, you can't deny that.' He feels a great emotion welling in his chest.

He doesn't know what it is but it might make him cry soon. 'I didn't have to help you, but I did. Nearly got myself beat up. Talked to by the police. Now you're laughing at me. That's not nice. You shouldn't be doing that.'

Dan shrugs. 'Okay. I can't tell you anything because I don't know. It's just that Jimmy's in for a surprise.'

'What's that mean?'

Dan shrugs again. 'I don't know. He'd just better watch his ginger arse.'

Pedlar John shrinks back from the table. All of a sudden he can't hear any noise in the pub. He doesn't know what to do. He quite likes Dan but he's afraid of the Twins. And he's afraid of Dan's dad.

Dan leans forward and pokes a finger at him. He's quite drunk now. 'What's Little Jimmy gonna say about that, eh?'

Suddenly decided, he stands up. 'Got to go to the toilet,' he says. Dan nods and leans back in his chair.

He weaves through the crowd at the bar and goes through the door to the Gents. There's a corridor with doors for male and female toilets. He pushes into the male toilet and opens his phone and calls.

'Yeah, it's me. Yeah.'

He listens, nodding, wanting to get on but knowing he's got to be polite.

'Yeah, I know, I know,' he says. 'Listen, something's going on. Something's going to happen to Jimmy. That Dyke character has set something up ... '

Back in the bar, Dan seems more sober. He watches Pedlar John come back and sit down. Those eyes again, watching him.

'What's up?' he says, not sure he wants to know the answer.

Dan shakes his head. 'Nothing. Thinking about friendship, that's all.'

John brightens. 'Yeah, I'll drink to that!'

He lifts his drink but Dan looks away and says nothing.

CHAPTER FORTY-ONE

The lights in Jimmy's house were the only illumination in that part of the street. At one o'clock in the morning we'd expected pitch black, but something was wrong. Bedroom lights and downstairs lights blazed through windows where curtains remained open. The original plan had been for us to break in, disable Jimmy and any of his henchmen who were around, then ransack the place for evidence. Now we'd had to reconsider.

The eight of us in the black SUV leaned our heads together. Thompson and his men wore black jump-suits and balaclavas. I wore my leather jacket and a pained expression. We'd been watching for twenty minutes and I had a bad feeling.

Thompson looked at his watch. 'OK. Dex and Dorian, front and centre. Jeff and Two-eyes round the back. Slim, stay with the van. Jacob, you're on comms at the front. Dyke and I will follow the point.'

I wondered briefly why one of the men was called Two-eyes but thought it was the wrong time to ask.

'Remember,' Thompson said. 'My daughter could be in there. You don't shoot unless you're a hundred and ten percent sure. And not even then unless you're two feet from the target.'

The men nodded and adjusted their positions. At a signal, Dexter carefully opened the rear door and the men slithered out of the car like a multi-headed creature, barely making a sound as they hit the road. Jeff and Two-eyes broke into a trot and headed down the lane to come in from the back. We'd looked at maps across my kitchen table earlier and worked out how to get through the neighbour's garden and into Little Jimmy's. The two men had stared at the map for five minutes and hadn't looked at it since. They had it memorised, I guess.

Thompson held my arm before I climbed from the van. 'Time to step back, if you want,' he said.

I looked at his hand on my arm. 'Don't get in my way,' I said. 'This is my case, not yours.'

'And she's my daughter.'

'So let's go see if she's in there.'

He gripped me tighter. 'Tell me one more time why we're doing this.'

'Because I have absolutely no evidence that would interest the police. And besides, I think they've got their own agenda going for the Twins.'

'Which we're about to royally fuck up.'

'As you said, it's your daughter. And she might be in there.'

He paused a moment, then let go. We slid from the van and ran across the road. Dexter and Dorian had scaled the wall and Dexter was now playing with the lock on its other side. As we arrived, the gate gave a click and opened. He gave Thompson a thumbs-up, then turned and ran across the gravel towards the front door. Dorian was already there, head bowed over the lock. Thompson and I ran towards him.

Jimmy's red Corvette was gone from its parking space in front of the garage to the left. My bad feeling got worse.

The front door swung open and Dorian caught it. He and Dexter crouched low, nodded to each other, then pushed the door slowly inwards. The wide entrance slowly came into view, fully lit.

'Too easy,' I said quietly. The others turned to me, frowning. I'd broken a secret spy regulation. I pointed. 'There's an alarm panel there and it didn't go off.'

Dorian ran across the tiles to the kitchen door. When he was there, he pressed himself against the wall and watched Dexter join him. Thompson and I edged sideways into the entrance hall and looked on. Dorian leaned against the wall and reached out a hand, then pushed the door open. Dexter crouched again and ran inside. We saw him look around, then stand upright. He looked towards Thompson and lifted his chin briefly. I could almost hear him saying, 'Clear!' in his head, like they did in the cop shows.

It was so quiet I heard the soft tinkle of glass breaking in the kitchen. Dexter crouched and looked towards the back door, then relaxed and stood up as Jeff and Two-eyes came in.

They all looked at me.

I pointed towards the door that led to the lounge and Dexter and Dorian went through the same routine, emerging a moment later making hand signals that I guessed meant the room was empty.

Thompson pointed upstairs and the four musketeers trotted up. I hadn't been upstairs on my previous visit so thought it might be worthwhile to go. By the time I reached the top, the four of them had entered two of the bedrooms, which also seemed to be lit.

I was standing waiting for them to come out when the bedroom door to my right opened and Mikey emerged, wearing only pyjama bottoms and looking bleary. A night-time visit to the toilet was about to turn bad for him. He was bruised by his left eye where Dan had kicked him. He saw me at once and tried to step back into his room but I was too quick. I pushed the door open and punched him square on the point of his jaw. His eyes rolled up and he began to fall. I caught him under the arms and lowered him down. I said, 'Sorry,' but I think he was already out by that time.

When I came back out, the four agents were standing applauding silently. I shrugged as if to say it was nothing.

Thompson was at the head of the stairs and he took the final bedroom, poking his head around the corner like a guest taking a quick tour and not expecting to find anything.

'Okay,' he said in his normal voice. 'Jeff tie up that man. There's obviously no one here but him. Anywhere else we can look, Dyke?'

'Follow me.'

I took them downstairs and through the door that led down again to the basement. I switched on the light and the others came in behind me. The dentist's chair was still in the centre of the room, its straps dangling. A shiver went through me as I remembered Little Jimmy's hands on my wrists, trying to hold me down so he could cut me.

'Geez, look at this,' Dexter said, pointing to the case of fingers harvested by Little Jimmy.

'He's a collector,' I said. 'Keeps him off the streets.'

We opened the cabinet doors and pulled out the drawers. We looked behind cupboards and tested all the fixtures and fittings for permanence. Nothing.

Jeff came down and looked around. His eyes lit up when

he saw the dentist's chair in the middle of the room.

'Wow, top of the range seat.' He noticed us looking at him. 'My dad was a dentist, what can I say?' He sat in the chair and it gave slightly.

I remembered something.

'Get off the chair,' I said.

'Okay, don't be— '

I took his shoulder and levered him off. He stood to his full height and was about to say something when I gave the chair a hard push. It rolled smoothly away, revealing a door underneath.

'Don't ask me how I knew,' I told them. 'I'd have to kill you.'

I reached down and pulled at the trap door. There was some kind of electronic locking mechanism but Jimmy must have forgotten to enable it because the door lifted easily. Another lighted room was visible beneath.

'Here,' Dorian said, carrying over a set of aluminium ladders that had been leaning against the wall and whose purpose now became obvious. We lowered them and I went down into the room. It was furnished with a bed, a table, some kitchen fitments and a sink. There was an expensive glass shower unit in one corner. It smelled of dirty clothing.

I felt someone come down behind me. Thompson stepped into the room. 'She was here,' he said.

'Yes.'

'The bastard kept her here.'

'This was his secret place,' I said. 'Where he kept things for himself.'

Thompson shook his head. When he spoke, his voice was hard. 'Where can we find this Wilder bastard?' he asked.

'At this moment, I don't know.'

He grabbed me by the arm again. 'You find him,' he said.

'Find him before I do. Because if I find him first, nobody else will.'

CHAPTER FORTY-TWO

We left Mikey where I'd dropped him and withdrew. Dorian switched off the lights and closed the door behind us.

There was silence in the van. Slim drove us carefully out of the area and back on to the M56, then headed towards Manchester airport. The men took off their overalls, unloaded their weapons, exchanged their boots for trainers. They began to joke amongst themselves as the tension dissipated.

'Next time,' Thompson said to me, 'make sure your intelligence is good.'

'They were warned,' I said.

'You think?'

'That's Jimmy's lair. He doesn't leave it unless he has to.'

'And the guy you cold-cocked?'

I shrugged. 'Human sacrifice. He didn't know we were coming. Meant to look like Jimmy didn't know either.'

'They left all the lights on. And the alarm switched off.'

'Maybe Mikey forgot. He's a villain, not a university professor.'

Thompson considered this. 'Who'd you tell?'

I looked him in the eye. 'No one. What about you?'

'Nobody who knows Wilder.'

The van pulled up outside the hotel on the airport where Thompson and his men had taken some rooms. They stashed their gear in large bags and jumped out of the van—to all intents a group of tourists who'd been seeing the fleshpots of Manchester.

Thompson took me to one side. 'These men have put in good time for me, with no return. I can't keep pulling favours.'

'I'll be in touch when I know more.'

'We'll be here another forty-eight hours. I can't hold them longer than that.'

He was still playing tough but his body language was dejected. He grabbed a bag from the back of the van then followed his men into the hotel. I found my car and tried to ring Dan but it was three-thirty in the morning and there was no reply. I hoped to God that whoever he'd told about the raid on Jimmy's hadn't ratted him out for his trouble.

In my dream I was running through a crowded city street. Everyone ignored me, turning away as I approached, grabbing their children and hurrying into shops. My feet hit the paving slabs in regular rhythm, as though I were beating out time for a tune that only I could hear. There was no one behind me, chasing. There was no one in front of me, hunted. But I had to keep running, shunting and weaving through armies of ordinary people performing their ordinary tasks, living their ordinary lives. The sound of my feet on the pavement grew louder, less regular, as if I were stumbling or tripping. And then it started coming in short bursts and took up a place in my head ...

I woke abruptly to the sound of loud knocking on my door. I looked at my clock—seven thirty. I'd been asleep less than three hours. Glancing out the window as I pulled on my jeans and sweat-shirt I noticed a dark Peugeot Boxer pulled up in front, its side door open. Moody.

The man Simms who'd kidnapped me outside Jimmy Wilder's house stood on my doorstep with another clone I didn't recognise. My life suddenly seemed full of athletic young men who could kill you with their little finger and I was getting tired of it.

'Your presence is requested,' Simms said without introduction.

'Tell Moody to go fuck himself.'

He raised an eyebrow. 'I've got instructions,' he said mildly. 'Don't make me comply.'

The other man snickered. Like Simms he wore a leather jacket over an open-necked check shirt. His Adidas sneakers looked brand new.

I said, 'And tell Dolly Parton here that I'll wipe that smile off his face if he giggles again.'

Simms took a calming breath and spread his hands. 'Look, don't play the hard-ass. It's just a conversation.'

'At this time in the morning?'

'Spring is in the air. Morning's the best time of the day. Come in and get it over with.'

I fetched my own leather jacket and climbed into the back of the Boxer. Unlike the one I'd travelled in the night before, which had smelled of machine oil and testosterone, this smelled of Armani's *Gio*. Our police have such good taste in after-shave.

To my surprise they drove me to a local police station. 'Mohammed comes to the mountain,' Simms said. 'Consider yourself honoured.'

Moody was patrolling an interview room, arms folded, lips pursed and brow furrowed. I sat in a chair and waited for him. I was past caring. I'd called Dan again but was re-directed to voice mail. I'd also begun to think about Kelly and her whereabouts, and whether our actions last night had put her in more danger.

All in all I was in no shape to deal with Moody and his extravagant gestures of irritation.

Finally he turned and stared at me directly. When he spoke he was obviously trying to contain himself.

'So, did your little jaunt get you anything?'

I gave him the blank eyes, just to see how mad he could get.

'You and your sporty chums had a great time,' he went on. 'Thought it was the Iranian Embassy all over again, did you? Black outfits, balaclavas, fancy shooters. Must have felt like you were on TV.'

'I take it there's a point to all this.'

He stood in front of me, his arms folded again. 'I was willing to give you some leeway, Dyke, because I thought we were on the same side. I thought we both wanted the Wilders to go down for the shitty stunts they pull.'

'Nothing's changed.'

'Really? Oh really? So what happened last night, then? Right little waltz of the toreadors, wasn't it?'

'You saw what happened.'

'You might think that. I couldn't possibly comment.'

He grabbed a chair and sat facing me.

I said, 'Your men were good. We didn't see them.'

'Which men was that?'

I stared at him. 'You were watching the house. You saw us arrive. So the question is, what else did you see?'

'Apart from a group of nonces ruining a perfectly good

observation?'

I began to realise something that Moody wasn't telling me. 'If you were watching us then you saw them. You saw Jimmy pack up and go.'

'Oh, so it's sharing information now, is it? You're happy for me to tell you what *I* was up to, though you had no intention of telling me what *you* were up to. I call that cheek. I might ask Simms to step in so we can have a really good laugh at that.'

'You or your men watched Jimmy wheel a car or a van or something up to the house and then leave. You sat and watched through your expensive telephoto lenses and did nothing. Fuck all.'

Moody's face began to develop ridges and humps like a bowl of soup beginning to boil. 'Do *not* talk to me like that.'

'Why not? I can talk to a clown how the hell I want. That's what clowns are for.'

He stood so quickly his chair fell backwards. 'I warned you about this, Dyke. I specifically warned you about getting in our way. And what did you do? Walked right into the frame and fucked up everything.'

I was shaking my head. 'You can't put this on me, Inspector. You watched the whole thing go down and did nothing.'

'Will you stop saying that? There were perfectly good reasons—'

'For watching a kidnapper spirit away his swag?'

He made a physical effort and calmed down. He looked at his watch and walked to the room's single window.

'If you'd been honest with me about your involvement in the beginning it might have been different.'

'I was protecting my client.'

He snorted. 'Bullshit. You wanted to be left alone, with us

out of the picture. All that nonsense about working for the residents' committee.'

'In a larger sense, I am.' I looked at his back. His shoulders were tense, his posture strained. I said, 'So who told you?'

He turned towards me. 'Thompson's not as clandestine an operator as he thinks he is. When he showed up at that girl's murder scene, word came back to me because I had a ticket on you. The local plod are cooperating with him but I've just taken a watching brief. I owe him nothing.'

I thought back to the night before. Everything we'd done had been observed by Moody or at least by his men, working on shift. They would have watched our silent break-in while holding back their tears of laughter, knowing that Little Jimmy had already flown.

'So when Jimmy left why didn't you follow him?'

He was quiet for a long while.

'We did follow him,' he said. 'Unfortunately, our paymasters don't always provide us with all the resources to make our job easier.'

'You didn't have the manpower.'

'You can only do so much with two men and a dog.'

I couldn't believe what I was hearing. 'Didn't it seem important to your guys when Jimmy's routine changed? They must have backed a car up to the house or something to get the girl inside—'

He raised a hand. 'You're talking as though I give a good goddamn about this girl, Dyke.'

'Excuse me. I thought kidnapping was still a serious crime.'

'It is. But so is smuggling.'

'What are you talking about? The Wilders are thugs and bullies. And I don't think anyone as secretive and important as you is interested in their drug smuggling activity. That's real police work for real policemen.'

'Who said anything about drugs? We're talking about diamonds. Uncut diamonds coming straight from the mines of Africa to your front door.'

CHAPTER FORTY-THREE

This one was struggling more than usual. Jimmy thought, serves me right for picking a young man. He should have been more careful.   He made a guttural noise as he gripped the dealer's hand more tightly. He was a black man in his mid-twenties and he was reasonably well-muscled, unlike most of the low-lifes he dealt with.

'Keep struggling, it gets worse,' he said. 'I'll take two 'stead of one.'

'Fuck off, you bastard,' the man said. 'Leggo me hand.'

'Got to pay the ferryman,' Jimmy said, working his snippers into position.

They were on a housing estate somewhere in south Manchester. He never really knew where he was, just followed directions. Sparkle had been good like that, kept him informed. Of course he was shit-scared, silly bugger. He was implicated in a murder now, so he had to look after Jimmy and make sure he got what he wanted. It wouldn't last, of course, and Jimmy would have to do something about him eventually. But for the moment he was happy to use him as a source of local knowledge of all things illegal or dodgy in Manchester.

This time he'd ended up in a lump of grey wasteland behind a row of council houses. At least he was getting around a bit, he thought, laughing grimly to himself, getting to see the world.

The man had found some extra strength and was pounding on Jimmy's back now, bringing a hard fist down repeatedly on his shoulders and neck. Jimmy took another breath and felt his muscles pump up. If he wanted it rough, he would get it rough. No problem.

Then the man started to laugh and stopped his beating. Jimmy became alert at once. Something had changed but he wasn't sure what. He relaxed his grip slightly and stood up, though he twisted the man's arm enough to force him sideways to the floor.

He heard it, then. A distant two-tone wail of a police car on its way. That's why the man started laughing—he thought he was about to be saved.

Jimmy spun round, continuing to twist the man's arm so that he fell even further to the floor. His hair was in corn-rows and a gold tooth glinted in his mouth as he grimaced. Jimmy felt the sharp edge of the man's large ring under his fingers.

He said, 'What's your name?'

'Wha'?'

'I said what's your name?'

'Hear them bells, man. We got lookouts now. You been rumbled. The filth gonna wipe your arse!'

Jimmy twisted the man's wrist almost to the point of breaking. He squealed and rolled to escape the pain.

'Matty!' he said, almost breathless. 'Matty! Matthew's my name but they call me Matty.'

Jimmy pulled upwards so that the man was kneeling in front of him. He shifted his fingers on the cutters so that the blades were together, forming a sharp point.

'Good, Matty. Well done. You saved a finger.'

'Good for me, hey?'

'Almost,' Jimmy said, and drove the closed blades of the secateurs into Matty's chest. He felt the ribs cave in beneath the force of the blow. The man's expression was shocked for a second, then his eyes rolled upwards and he sagged backwards. Jimmy released his wrist and he fell to the ground. Shit, that felt good. *Now* he would go.

He walked quickly back through the streets to where the Corvette was parked underneath a street lamp. He didn't like leaving it in such an obvious place, but he wanted to deter thieves by putting it in a well-lit spot. He climbed inside and drove away, peeling off his gloves as he manoeuvred the car through the drab streets.

Pete was on his mind all the time now. As usual, he'd turned out to be ahead of the game. Jimmy had been at home watching TV yesterday when Pete had rung.

'Get the fuck out,' was the first thing he'd said. 'The bizzies are on their way. You let that bitch go, didn't you?'

Jimmy ignored the question. He'd told Pete days ago that he'd released Kelly. Got him off his back. But this could be tricky.

He said, 'What's going on?'

'Little birdie,' Pete laughed, sounding cocky now because he knew something Jimmy didn't.

'What little birdie?'

'Never you mind. Clean your place up. Paperwork, cash, everything. Leave Mikey. Don't tell him anything. They'll think you didn't know they were coming.'

'You winding me up?'

'Okay, never mind me. Put your feet up and wait for the knock on the door.'

So he'd opened up the hatch and brought Kelly out. She was scared but he told her not to worry, he wasn't going to hurt her.

'How do I know that?' she said, standing with her weight on one leg and staring at him. 'You could be lying. That's all you do, is lie. And you're crap at it. You big fat liar.'

He'd slapped her then, just to keep her quiet. He didn't like doing it but it did feel good. He'd known it was coming on for a while so it was good to get it out.

He told Mikey to fetch his car in. Mikey had a big Land Rover Defender that they'd backed up to the front of the house. He'd put tape around Kelly's mouth and taped her hands behind her, then he'd picked her up over his shoulder and dumped her in the back of the car. Plus two boxes of papers and other bits and bobs. It was nearly midnight so nobody was around, not that they could see over the walls anyway.

'What do I do?' Mikey said.

'Play with yourself,' Jimmy told him. 'Use the TV, take a shit, I don't care. I'll be back tomorrow for the car. Don't go anywhere.'

'Where are you going? What's happening?'

'I'm just having a clear out. Blame Pete, he's nervous. Call my mobile if you must. Don't answer to Pete if he calls. Let me deal with him.'

Then he'd driven away.

Now it was twenty-four hours later and he needed to check everything was still okay. He and Pete had kept the house after they'd done it up. It was one of the first they'd renovated and they decided it would be good to have an alternative address in case they needed it later. It was round the corner from where they used to live when they were kids. They'd put good strong locks on it so that you could lock up from outside, and they made sure it always had some tins and long-life milk in the cupboards. They'd never had to use it till now, but it was good to have a back-up.

Jimmy left the car down the street in the lock-up garage that came with the house. The street brought back memories—him and Pete running wild, pushing kids up against the sides of houses and asking for money. Him and Pete climbing walls and breaking into conservatories just to piss in the plants. Games of football with all the other kids scared of them and not wanting to tackle properly for fear of upsetting them. Everything had gone right for them when they were nippers. They never had any money, but it was still fun to look out for yourself, to have others be afraid of you and keep out of your way.

Now he was grown up it was all hard work. Mind your manners. Keep the tax man happy, do things properly ... At least, make it look like that. Which made it twice as hard work. Good job Pete was crafty like that. Jimmy resented the fact that Pete was always the one with the plans—but he knew Pete was clever enough to make sure they were both safe. He'd always looked after both of them. Jimmy had bulked up as a way of going one better than his brother. But he knew where the real power was.

They'd made sure the street lamp near the safe house was always broken, keeping it dark outside the house at all times. Even so, as Jimmy came close he could tell something was wrong. The front door was slightly ajar. He slowed down and looked around. Just one car, parked thirty yards down the street. No one else on the street. Lights showing in most of the windows, behind curtains. The blue glare of television screens flickering in the front rooms of the people who had no idea that the Wilder Twins were neighbours.

He swung open the low wooden gate and walked up the path, gripping the snippers inside his jacket pocket. It was quiet inside so he could hear his own footsteps on the concrete. He'd left Spud in charge—he thought that dumb arsehole could just about manage looking after a skinny girl locked in a room. He'd given him a pile of magazines and his PSP to keep him occupied, and told him not to move. If he needed anything, he was to call.

So an open front door was not a good sign.

As he got to the door he reached out and pushed it further open, on to the dark hallway. He stepped through, then halted, bringing his snippers out. Spud was inside, sitting on the floor with his arms tied behind him and grey Duck tape wrapped over his mouth and round the back of his head. Trussed up like a turkey ready for Christmas. He looked up when Jimmy entered, then looked away.

But he hadn't looked away, Jimmy realised. He'd pointed with his eyes towards the stairs. Jimmy was turning to look when he heard a voice.

'Stand still,' the voice said.

Jimmy saw then that Kelly was half-way down the stairs, looking scared and not very sure of her footing. In front of her, facing him, was the young boy—Dyke's kid. Dan. That was it.

He breathed out. This was going to be all right then. He took a step forward.

'I said stand still!' the boy shouted, and there was something in his voice that pulled Jimmy up short. That's when he noticed that the kid had a shooter, and it was pointing straight at him.

'All right,' he said. 'I heard you the first time. I was just getting comfortable.'

'Don't bother,' Dan said. He seemed confident, which put Jimmy on edge. The boy came down another step, bringing Kelly with him.

'You're not going anywhere, sunshine,' Jimmy said. 'Not with her.'

Dan took a further step down the stairs. They were narrow and without a banister rail, but he seemed well-balanced.

Jimmy was struck by something. 'Hey, how did you find this place?' he asked.

Dan grinned. 'A big red Defender is easy enough to follow,' he said. 'Don't you ever use your rear-view mirror?'

'Clever little bastard, aren't you? You and your dad together. We'll have to pay you another visit, see if we can't knock some of those brains out of you.'

Jimmy liked that. He wasn't good at repartee normally but he was beginning to feel smart. After all, he'd caught them before they got away, hadn't he?

Dan had reached the bottom step. In one hand he held the gun that was still pointing at Jimmy. The other was behind him, holding Kelly by the wrist. Now he waved the gun, ushering Jimmy away from the door. Jimmy planted his feet, waiting for a moment when he could reach and grab the girl.

'You reckon I'm moving?' he asked. 'What makes you think that?'

Dan sighed as if he were losing patience with an older person. 'You probably don't use guns much, do you?' he said. 'Haven't seen the damage they can do. This one's a Desert Eagle, manufactured by Israel Military Industries. It comes in a variety of calibres—this particular one happens to be a Magnum 44. The pressure it generates inside the barrel means that it can't use lead bullets—they're too soft. So imagine the kind of bullets it has to use in order to work properly. And imagine the damage a bullet that hard will do going through your guts. It'll make a hole about two inches wide.'

Jimmy focused on the end of the gun barrel. He knew from what Mikey had said that this kid knew ju-jitsu or something—perhaps he wasn't such a soft touch after all. Still and all, he was quick on his feet and could probably snatch Kelly when they went past.

He shifted his head slightly to look at her. She was still standing behind Dan even though they had both reached the bottom of the stairs.

'Kelly,' he said. 'You're not going to go with this kid, are you? You didn't understand the plans I had.'

Her head came up and a fire suddenly entered her eyes. 'Plans?' she said. 'What plans were those, you moron? You *kidnapped* me! You think I was gonna walk down the aisle with you or something?'

Dan put his arm out. 'Easy, Kel. Don't let him get to you.'

But before he or Jimmy could stop her, she'd taken a step forward and slapped Jimmy hard across the face.

'Motherfucker! Get out of the way!'

Jimmy was stunned. He hadn't seen it coming – she'd been as quick as a snake. He hadn't even put his hands up. And before he knew what he was doing he had made a sideways move, away from the door. He stepped over Spud, who had his head on his chest as if he were trying not to be seen.

'I didn't explain meself,' Jimmy said, and heard the plea in his voice. He hated himself for it but for the first time in a long while he felt a real emotion ... some kind of tightness in his chest. It made his eyes well up. That fucker Dan was going to pay for this.

Kelly must have seen Jimmy's face and she became even bolder. She strode ahead of Dan and opened the door. 'Oh, for fuck's sake,' she said. 'Come on, Dan. Get me out of here before he starts blubbering.'

The door slammed shut and Jimmy felt the heat drain out of his body. He didn't understand why but he didn't even want to go to the door and run after them. He stood there for a moment with conflicting emotions running back and forth in his head. Then he looked down at Spud and kicked him once. 'You useless piece of shite,' he said.

Then he went through into the living room and began to systematically tear it apart.

CHAPTER FORTY-FOUR

They say the sun shines on the good and the wicked alike, though I like to think that's a calumny spread by the bad guys trying to take credit for good weather.

The next morning I rose to Spring sunshine which did little to lighten my mood. I did my five miles, then drove into the office. People were smiling. Offices were glistening in the morning light. Things were looking good ... And I still felt bad.

But what did I have to be happy about? The Wilders seemed to be getting away with something, though we weren't sure what. My son wasn't answering my calls. Laura answered the phone, said she was all right, then went back to work as quickly as she could. And I had no leads on Kelly. Nothing. Where was she now? What was happening to her? What would those bastards do to her if they thought she was the cause of all their problems?

I stopped myself thinking along those lines. It was too maddening to think of the Wilders with her, even though I'd never met the girl. It twisted a knife in my gut.

I could go and sit outside the Wilders' offices, or their homes, but what good would that achieve if they knew they were being watched? If they had any sense – a bit of a stretch, admittedly – they'd pull up the drawbridge and lay low for a week or two, until the coppers' attention went elsewhere. I stared out of my office window and wondered why I didn't know what to do next.

Well that was true until 11.05, when Laura knocked once and then walked straight in.

'Light of my life,' I said.

'Have you seen Dan?'

'Not since the day he was released. He didn't seem happy with me so I haven't pushed it. He's not answering my calls.'

She sat down on one of my two chairs. She was wearing her office suit with the wide-lapelled yellow shirt beneath it. It showed off her collar-bone, one of her best features.

She said, 'He came back with me to work that afternoon. We went home that night and he asked if he could borrow the car.'

'I didn't even know he could drive.'

'He showed me his licence. I'm not that stupid.'

'So did he bring it back?'

She drew a deep breath. 'He didn't come back at all, with or without the car. I thought he'd be out celebrating with friends or something, so I didn't do anything. But it's been two days now and I'm worried.'

'Didn't you think to tell me?'

She waved a hand as if dismissing a fly. 'You'd only get worried—or angry. You're not exactly Mr Calm these days.'

'There isn't a lot to be calm about, is there? When you find out your only son is banged up on suspicion it's hard to keep a lid on your emotions.'

'You manage it most of the time.'

'What's that supposed to mean?'

'You know what it means.'

'Just because I don't go around yelling at the top of my voice doesn't mean I'm calm.'

'Sam, I'm just saying it would be nice to know what you're feeling from time to time. That you *had* feelings, actually.'

I glanced through the window of my office at the people of Crewe going about their business in the morning sunshine. It didn't make me feel any better.

'Look,' she said. 'I know it's been hard for you to find out you're a dad. But you've known for almost four months and you did nothing about it until Dan turned up on your doorstep. You have to deal with these things—talk about them. Acknowledge your feelings.'

'Why? What good would it do? I still won't know how to be a proper father. Dan should live with you—you're a better mother than I am a father.'

'Don't be silly— '

'You're certainly showing him more attention than I am.'

'What do you mean? I'm only trying to help.'

'Well it's not working.'

'How dare you— '

She stood up and I could tell we were about to tip over a cliff, tumbling headlong into an argument that I knew was completely uncalled-for.

The Fates were on our side, though, because my office telephone chose that moment to ring. We both stared at it as though it had slapped us around the face. I picked it up.

'Hi, Dad,' Dan said. 'I thought I should give you a call. Write this down.' He read out the address of a hotel near Junction 20 of the M6. 'Get yourself up here and Kelly will tell you what's been going on.'

Laura had borrowed a company BMW so she drove while I phoned Kelly's father. He listened quietly while I told him what I knew.

'And she's safe?' he asked, his voice tight, as though his throat were constricted.

'As far as I know.'

He paused. 'Your boy?'

It came again—that strange feeling when someone talked about my 'boy'.

'He seemed OK too. We're about twenty minutes away.'

'We'll see you there.'

Laura had her eyes fixed on the motorway but she seemed to know exactly what I was thinking. 'Two dads,' she said. 'Worried about their kids. What a pair of hard-cases you are.'

'Are you suggesting I've got feelings? That's a turn-around.'

'I never suggested you didn't have them. I said you kept them to yourself.'

'Which is a Bad Thing.'

'Don't let's argue again. I can't keep it up.'

'Just because I argue better than you doesn't mean to say I'm right.'

Now she turned and gave me a sardonic look. 'What book did you read *that* in?'

I huffed. 'Wasn't a book. It was a play, actually.'

She took the slip road off the motorway and within five minutes we were bumping slowly over the traffic-calming humps at the entrance to the Thistle hotel. She parked in a bay and we walked through a pair of large glass doors into a dim reception and lobby. To one side a curving reception counter swept away from us. Through an opening I could see another lounge with a bar on its furthest wall. Closer to us, a dozen or so deep leather chairs were scattered about the lobby, and in two of them Dan and Kelly were seated, watching us calmly.

Dan introduced us to Kelly. She was thin and pale with blonde hair that fell to her shoulders. After the initial handshake she had difficulty meeting our gaze.

'We stayed here last night,' Dan said. 'Lucky to find a room. We pitched up at midnight like a couple of waifs and strays.'

'Must have cost,' I said.

'I put it on a credit card. I'm sure Kelly's dad will cover it.'

At the mention of her father, Kelly shivered. Dan noticed and covered her hand with his. 'Don't sweat it,' he said. 'You don't have to see him if you don't want.'

Laura and I exchanged a glance.

'He's on his way,' I said. 'Sorry. It seemed the right thing to do.'

Kelly looked up, startled. 'He's here? No way! I can't see him yet.'

Laura sat next to her and reached out a hand. 'Everyone was worried about you.'

'Well they had no right!' she said, withdrawing her hand. 'Jesus, I can't get away from anyone, can I?'

Dan seemed to take this personally. He shifted backwards in his chair.

'So can you tell me what happened?' I asked, trying to distract her. 'Why were you taken?'

Kelly looked at Dan, who shrugged. I guess that meant I was OK to talk to. Kelly leaned back and looked up at the ceiling of the ornate lobby.

'That big bastard,' she began.

'Jimmy Wilder?'

'Yeah, he's the one. One of those guys with a neck thicker than the top of his pointy head. We were at a party way over towards Liverpool somewhere ... I don't even know where we were, Jesus. Me and some of the girls ... Close your ears, Dan.'

'It's OK.'

She shrugged. 'We went out as the entertainment but I got hit on straight away by this big fucker. Wouldn't take no for a fuck off, would he? But he was flashing his wallet, big rolls of cash. So I thought, hey, take advantage. If the guy's got a hard-on for you, make it work.'

'But something went wrong.'

'Good guess, Dan's dad. Jimmy and his brother got in an argument with this skinny guy with a big nose. I didn't want to hear what they were saying but I couldn't help it, they were so loud. Then the brother, Pete, he noticed me and starts walking towards me. So then Jimmy stands in his way and tells him to calm down, but then *he* grabs me by the arms and takes me downstairs and throws me in this ... This *dungeon*.'

'I've seen it,' I said.

'Yeah, but you haven't *lived* in it, have you? Weeks of microwave slop, underwear that don't fit, nothing to read, crappy music to listen to. My God, I didn't even have *cable*.'

I saw Laura's eyebrows go up a fraction before she got them under control.

I said, 'So what was it you overheard? Can you remember?'

'Nothing!' she said. 'Big fat zero. I was out of it, stoned and drunk. Even if I heard anything I don't remember it. But could I tell that to big boy? Oh, no. I had to be his little plaything, didn't I?'

'So you have no idea what they were talking about?'

She sighed and stared upwards again. 'All I remember is the nerdy-looking guy was going crazy. He kept saying, "I can't do it, I can't do it." Swear to God, that's all I heard. I have no idea what he was talking about.'

'That's OK,' I told her. 'I know what it means.'

'Well jolly good show. Now can I get out of here before my illustrious pater turns up?'

'Where do you want to go?'

'Somewhere south, near the sun, please God.'

We all stood up, but I saw Kelly's expression change as she looked past me. Turning, I saw Brad Thompson walking through the glass doors, Dexter and Dorian moving behind him like black-suited guardian angels.

Thompson stopped and raised his arms as though he expected Kelly to run towards him and bury her head in his breast. From what I'd seen so far she was just as likely to jump through the plate glass window behind her.

But she surprised me. She wiped the palms of her hands on her legs and smiled dimly at him. 'Hi, Dad.'

Thompson lowered his arms and came closer. He hadn't acknowledged any of us yet. 'Hi, Baby. How are you doing?'

She shrugged. Then her eyes began to well up. 'Not good ... ' she began, and tears lipped over her eyelids and ran down her cheeks. Thompson went closer and put his arms around her, looking at us over the top of her head. His own eyes weren't entirely clear.

He held her at arm's length and spoke to her. 'Look, we're going home now. You can see your mom and we'll decide what's best to do next.'

She was nodding her head, her blonde hair moving up and down. I tried to catch Dan's eye but he was looking away, into the darkness of the foyer. I couldn't guess what he was thinking.

Thompson must have made a gesture, because Dorian had stepped forward and was offering a hand towards Kelly, who stepped away from her father without looking back at us. Thompson shook my hand, then looked at Dan.

'So you're the hero,' he said. 'What happened?'

Dan swallowed and explained that he'd followed Jimmy in the Land Rover to a house in Liverpool. He'd watched for a day to make sure that the goon known as Spud was by himself, then just knocked on the door.

'How did you know he was going to move Kelly?'

Dan looked at me. 'I didn't. Just dumb luck I happened to be there to see it happen.'

'Okay. So you knocked on the door and Spud answered.'

'Dan knows Tae Kwon Do,' I said, sounding like a proud father.

'I get it. You overpowered him, then what?'

Dan shrugged. 'Kelly was locked in a room upstairs. I managed to kick the door in, and I was just bringing her downstairs when Jimmy walked in.'

Laura's hand went up to her mouth. 'Did he see you?'

'Yeah, but I had a secret weapon.'

He reached behind him on the chair into a grey haversack and pulled out the fake Desert Eagle he'd used on me when he first walked into my office.

'Whoa,' Thompson said, and took the replica from Dan's outstretched hand.

Dan said, 'It's OK. It's a BB gun. Cost me £30 on the internet. Looks good, though, doesn't it?'

'Isn't there some law against those?' Laura asked, her eyes wide.

Dan shrugged. 'As long as you're seventeen you can buy them.'

Thompson handed the gun back. 'Well you're a creative little bastard, I'll give you that.'

'What will happen with Kelly?' I asked.

Thompson looked over towards her. She was talking to Dorian, who was smiling at what she was saying.

'I think we'll go back to the States,' Thompson said. 'Her mom's not happy here and I'm told there's an office waiting for me.'

Dan spoke up. 'Can I ... '

'What?'

'Can I have a word with her before you go?'

Thompson smiled for the first time in the days I'd known him. 'Sure. Swap email addresses, whatever.'

Dan stood and went over to Kelly. He tapped her on the shoulder and she turned. They walked further into the foyer while we all watched.

'Poor kids,' Thompson said. 'They're never gonna see each other again.'

'You sound sure about that.'

He turned towards me, his eyes cold. 'Oh yeah, I'm sure about that.'

Laura and I were silent on the drive home. We'd agreed to let Dan drive her car back so that he could have some time by himself. He'd waved at Kelly as she'd climbed into her father's car, then he simply turned and told us he'd make his own way back. We didn't have the heart to argue.

Now Laura was driving and I was looking out of the side window at the traffic.

I said, 'Dan told Pedlar John that something was going to happen.'

She looked sidelong at me. 'How do you know?'

'I let it slip on the phone the night before. He must have

told Pedlar John, who told Jimmy or Pete. That's why the house was empty when we got there.'

'But why would he do that?'

'Yes, that's certainly one of the questions. Maybe he was testing John. Testing his friendship.'

'And he failed.'

'Terminally.'

'And then what … he took my car and went and watched Little Jimmy's place, on the off chance?'

'Little blighter had it all planned.'

'But it worked out well for you. What if they'd all been there when you turned up?'

I sighed. 'It might have been messy. But we might have found Kelly earlier.'

'She was found anyway,' Laura pointed out. 'Not that she seemed particularly grateful.'

I was about to defend Kelly's attitude when my mobile phone rang. It was Trevor Clarke, sounding excited.

'Developments, my boy, developments,' he said breathlessly.

'You bought a new jacket?'

He cackled. 'Nice one. No, it's about Addison. He didn't turn up for work today, did he? How do I know that, I hear you ask? Well, I telephoned him as part of my usual badgering routine and got through to the gatekeeper in his office. And blow me down, she was quite flustered. He wasn't in work but no one knew where he was. He wasn't officially on leave and he wasn't answering any phones. I tell you, Sammy, something's happening.'

'You're leaping to a few conclusions there, Trevor. He can't have been missing long.'

'Maybe, maybe,' he conceded. 'But there are other factors.'

'Such as?'

'The Wilder twins are on the move. They've just taken some office space in Manchester and taken a lease on a big warehouse, too.'

'How do you know all this?'

He laughed again. He was enjoying himself. 'They always use the same agency. I have a mole who tips me the wink whenever they do something property-related. Earns himself a few quid.'

'So you think they're getting serious?'

'Oh yes. Now they've got the Dorset estate signed off they're probably feeling their oats. Bigger things on the horizon.'

Yes, I thought—and perhaps a diamond as big as the Ritz.

CHAPTER FORTY-FIVE

By the time Laura had dropped me off and I'd picked up my own car and driven to Liverpool it was late afternoon. The weather had been unseasonably bright and warm for a few days and the sun threw long shadows across the street where Addison's mother lived. I'd reasoned that if Addison had gone missing, then this might be his first hiding place.

I knocked on the door but there was no reply. I stepped to the side and peered through the lace-curtained windows, then knocked on the glass.

Still she didn't answer.

The door was an old fashioned affair with a Yale lock and a turn handle. Out of desperation I turned the handle – and the door pushed inwards. The Yale must have been stuck on its latch. I looked behind me at the street, then went in.

'Hello?' I said, raising my voice so it would travel through the whole house. No reply.

The stairs were straight ahead of me, with two doors off to the left – the sitting room where I'd talked to her before, then the dining room, and finally a kitchen at the back.

I didn't need to go that far. The sitting room was all I needed to see.

I sensed it before I even went inside, but I made myself do it. There was a different kind of stillness in the air. An absence of life. And a smell that is unmistakeable, once you've been exposed to it. I said, 'Hello?' again then pushed the door inwards.

I'd hoped not to find the scene but there it was. Mother and son. She laid out on the sofa, her legs up as though she were about to watch television but her eyes instead staring blankly at the ceiling, her white hair tumbling back over the arm of the sofa, her mouth open as if she might snore and wake up. Addison was seated facing her though he too was lolling to one side. It looked like Jimmy had tried to seat him upright but given up.

They both had huge, glistening wounds in the front of their bodies. Jimmy must have plunged his secateurs into their chests and killed them instantly. The blood had pumped out, soaked their clothing, then dripped down onto the edge of the chintz furniture and started to puddle and stain the carpet. The smell was dark and overpowering.

Without stepping further into the room I inspected it as best as I could. There was no message, no sign, nothing that might indicate Jimmy had wanted to leave his mark for others to see. This was pure brutality – he could do it, so he did.

To make sure Addison came, Jimmy must have forced his mother to phone him, asking him to come over on some pretence. Then he killed her. And as soon as Addison was in the house, Jimmy killed him too.

Sometimes you come across those like Jimmy who find that their power and strength gives them authority over others. But they only know they have that power when they exercise it. If they don't, then their sense of themselves wanes and dies.

So they constantly find ways to justify exercising their strength. They take offence easily. They invent imagined slights. They build their self-love to such an extent that it can never be questioned, because to question it is to question their whole identity.

Perhaps I'd started the process by getting in his face when he thought he had everything covered. Perhaps Dan had continued the rot by taking Kelly from him.

What was certain was that Jimmy's sense of himself was collapsing entirely. And that I and those that I loved were likely to be in the firing line.

CHAPTER FORTY-SIX

I made it to Laura's in record speed. I had no evidence to suggest Jimmy would go for her before looking for Dan. But I reckoned Jimmy was a coward at heart so he'd try the easy target first. And Dan had a better chance of looking after himself.

It was still light but the street lamps were flickering on as I pulled up outside. The company BMW was parked there but her own car wasn't in the driveway—she'd probably loaned it to Dan again. She was generous like that.

There was one other car in the street. A bright red Corvette. There was no one inside it.

I climbed out of my car, ducked low behind the hedge and ran towards the entrance to her driveway. Peering around, I saw that the front door was slightly ajar. Jimmy had probably pushed it in with a heave of his shoulders.

I hunkered down and listened. Just the occasional sound of a car whisking by into Tarvin, the village where Laura lived. No screams, no shouts, no sound of furniture breaking.

I looked at the distance between where I crouched and her front door—fifteen yards of crunchy gravel. No way around it or over it. No way around the back. It had to be a frontal assault.

Taking in three short breaths to inflate my lungs I stood and ran full-tilt towards the door, hearing my every step crash into the pea-shell. I hesitated only briefly at the door, then walked straight in.

The door gave directly on to Laura's lounge. Because of the low sun, it was dark in there. But I quickly saw her, sitting upright on her leather sofa. Little Jimmy Wilder was standing behind her, one hand on top of her head, the other holding a thirteen-inch machete blade against her neck. She had a bruised eye and she looked at me defiantly, directing her anger at Jimmy towards me.

'About time you got here,' Jimmy said. 'We were getting tired, weren't we, love?'

Laura twisted her head away from his hand but he grabbed it again. He wore a short brown leather jacket over his customary black tee-shirt. He must have changed since murdering the Addisons because there was no sign of blood on him.

'So what's the plan?' I asked. 'Snip our fingers off for your collection and then hope everything goes away?'

He let a smile touch his lips.

'You're a smart-arse, aren't you? Always with the clever talk. I like that.'

'We always like what we can't have.'

'Sam!' Laura said. She didn't want me to provoke him but it was the only weapon I had. Steroids seemed to have clouded his judgement to the point where he wasn't thinking about consequences any more. I had to get him around the sofa and coming towards me, otherwise he would just keep the upper hand by holding on to Laura.

'I found Addison,' I told him. 'I've reported it to the police and given them your name. It's all crashing around your thick ears, Jimmy. Pete's not going to be very pleased.'

He shrugged, causing Laura to stretch her neck away from the blade. 'Why should I give a shit what Pete thinks?'

'Pete's the one with the plans, isn't he? Smuggling diamonds and so on. How will you get on without his help?'

His smile disappeared. He didn't know we knew about the diamonds. He said, 'I don't need his help. I manage.'

'I can see that. Really on top of everything, aren't you?'

'Come here, you fucker—'

He moved the machete from Laura's neck and she rolled forward immediately, landing on the carpet on all fours and then rising to a crouch. She looked at me even as Jimmy came round the side of the sofa.

'Go!' I said, and she ran to the kitchen.

I retreated a step. Jimmy moved the machete back and forth in front of me so that it caught the last of the sun's rays and glinted threateningly. It looked new but it was small compared to some of the monsters I'd collected when I worked for Customs Excise. It would carve me up nicely nonetheless.

He was enjoying himself now, doing something he thought he was good at. 'Come on then, Mr Clever Dick,' he said. 'Think you can hack it? Eh?'

'Good joke, for an overweight freak with the brains of the Hulk.'

'Keep talking. I like it when they keep talking.'

'Yeah, Kelly told us all about you. All you could do was talk. She got bored, though. Tired of being the little princess to your Prince Charming.'

His face darkened. 'You shut up about her.'

'Oops, touched a nerve, have I?'

Dimly I heard Laura talking in the kitchen, probably calling the police.

As if seeing I was distracted, Jimmy lunged forward, slicing down with the machete. I'd been waiting for the lunge and I stepped backwards again, up against an upright piano that Laura had told me was a family heirloom. She had nowhere else to put it. On the top of its polished surface there were two brass candlesticks, with spikes in the centre for impaling candles. I grabbed one as I stepped backwards.

Now we faced each other, machete to candlestick. We were as even a match as I was going to get with a knick-knack.

Jimmy laughed out loud. 'Think that's gonna hurt?' he asked.

'Let's see,' I said. I feinted as if to strike from the left, backhanded, so that he brought his right hand up in defence, using the machete to stop my blow. Even as he started to grin, I surprised him and forced the machete down with the candlestick and stepped in close, smashing him on the nose with my left hand. Not my strongest hand, but hard enough to break the bones.

'Good move,' he said, raising his hand to feel the bridge of his nose.

'I'm full of them,' I said, and stepped in again, before he was set. I turned the candlestick and stabbed him twice quickly in the chest, through his black tee-shirt. The spike of the candlestick wasn't long, but was enough to break the skin and penetrate half an inch or so. He was quick enough to bring his right hand down again, the machete making a flashing arc, and I felt a nick as it sliced through my jacket and caught my arm. But now the machete was down low I reached over and held his arm with my left hand and punched him twice in the face with the butt of the candlestick. I wasn't having an impact on his weight-lifter's body, but his face was vulnerable.

He staggered back and looked down at his tee-shirt, where blood was starting to seep through.

'You little bastard,' he mumbled through his hand, which he'd brought up to his face.

I glanced past him to see Laura come back into the room.

'The police are on their way,' she said breathlessly.

Jimmy turned slowly to look at her. His eyes looked her up and down as though he hadn't really seen her before.

'You're a good 'un, aren't you?' he said. 'Thought you'd run away. Kelly should have had your brains 'stead of getting herself in trouble.'

He lowered his machete and stumbled forwards. But he was going past me to the outside. I let him go.

'This ain't over,' he said, and went out. A few moments later I heard the Corvette roar into life and drive off, tyres squealing.

Laura and I looked at each other. I went to her and put my arms around her. She allowed herself to be held for a moment, then pulled away and sat down heavily on the sofa.

'You're bleeding,' she said, nodding towards my arm. A thin line of red was showing through the slit in my jacket.

'I can't feel it,' I said.

'You'd best wash it.'

'I will.'

We looked at each other.

'I can't take much more of this, Sam,' she said. 'I don't feel safe anywhere.'

'I'll sort it out,' I said.

'Will you?' she said, suddenly fierce. 'Will you fix it so we can have our lives back? So that your son is safe, so that I don't feel frightened ever again? Can you do that, Sam?'

I took off my jacket and held it over my arm, then sat in a chair facing her. 'This isn't the life I have, Laura. I don't want it like this.'

'It might not be the life you want, but it's what you've got. And I don't know if I want it as well.'

The silence hung in the air for a minute, then I stood. 'I need to check Dan's OK.'

She looked away. 'I lent him my car until tomorrow. He said he was going home to sleep.'

I nodded then took out my mobile and rang him. He answered on the first ring, as if he were wired to it. I explained what had just happened with Little Jimmy. I asked him where he was.

'Just out,' he said. 'Couldn't sleep.'

'OK. Stay out till later.'

'So now what?' he asked.

'The police are on their way.'

'But you're not going to leave it at that, are you?'

'That's none—'

'Of my business. I get the picture. But you won't let them get away with that, attacking Laura. I'm getting to know you. You'll be after blood.'

'You don't know me at all,' I said. I hesitated. 'Look, I just wanted to say that I admire what you did for Kelly. You were bloody stupid to do it, but it took guts and you got away with it.'

He was quiet. 'I've been thinking,' he said at last.

'What about?'

'You and me.'

'What about us?'

'Perhaps we should work together, you know, like a team.'

I heard myself laughing before I knew I was doing it.

'You're joking, aren't you?'

'I think we'd be good together. I'm not cut out for clerical work. I've got street sense and I'm pretty handy—'

'You're eighteen years old.'

'I could be an Olympic boxing champion by now.'

'But you're not. I'm not going to talk about this, it's just too stupid.'

'Is that what you think?'

'That's what I think.'

'Okay.'

He hung up. I'd surpassed myself again. Pissed off two people in less than two minutes. Time to try for a third.

CHAPTER FORTY-SEVEN

This is more like it, Pedlar John thinks. Pete is finally appreciating what he'd done for him. Treated him nicely as soon as he knocked on the door. Asked him in, offered him a proper drink, not just coffee. It's as though all the tension has gone out of Pete. He's relaxed, cracking jokes. He still has his business head on, but he isn't quite so ... cruel.

They're sitting in Pete's lounge again, like they had last time. He thinks Marie is somewhere in the house, which he's always glad about, but he hasn't seen her. It's dark outside, and John can see the lights in the garden. Pete and Marie like their garden. It goes back for a couple of hundred feet, and there are little clusters of trees, and a big chalet thing, and statues every now and then with a light pointing up at it. You can't see it all from the house because it has nooks and crannies where it doubles back on itself, and if you walk around you find a garden seat or an archway with a swing in it. Pete had shown him the layout the first time he'd been asked to come and visit.

He's feeling okay, but he wishes Pete would stop asking

questions about Dan and his old man. Hasn't he given him all the information he had? What more can he say? He hasn't seen Dan since they left the pub together the other night, and he has no idea what Sam Dyke is doing. Doesn't care, either.

Pete is sitting in his big chair, the one in front of his plasma screen, and he's leaning back, holding a glass of whisky. John is holding the same thing, although his glass is just about empty. Pete is talking about his brother.

'I think the steroids have fucked him up,' he says. 'I never see him, and when I do he acts sneaky, as if he's hiding something from me.'

John moves uncomfortably in his seat. He knows Pete is asking him for information, but he doesn't have anything on Jimmy.

'What do you think?' Pete asks him. 'Do you think he's acting weird?'

'I don't know, Pete. I never see him these days. I don't know what he's up to.'

Pete nods, accepting this. 'You're right. The little fucker's never about. And it's not as if we haven't got things to do.'

'You mean like the building work, that new estate?'

Pete grins at him. 'Amongst other things. But I can't tell you about that, can I, 'cos I'd have to kill you.'

He says it with a smile but John feels a chill in his guts. He realises that he doesn't know why he's here. Usually when Pete asks him to visit, he gets straight down to business and then kicks him out. This time he's going all around the houses.

He plucks up the courage, and says, 'So what was it you wanted, Pete? I can get the last train back if I'm quick.'

Pete puts down his drink and points at him. 'You're empty, my man. Come through.'

He stands up and beckons John to follow. They walk out

of the lounge and turn left into the kitchen. John says, 'No, honest, Pete, I don't need another. This one's gone to me head as it is.'

But Pete has already opened a new bottle and is gesturing for him to come closer.

As he pours, he says, 'The problem, John, is that I can't trust anyone. Know what I mean?'

'Not sure I do.' His voice echoes in the tiled kitchen.

'Everyone around me is turning flaky. Not focused on the bigger picture. Looking out for themselves and satisfying their own needs. It's not good, John, it's not good.'

John makes his face look serious but he's aware that Pete is standing very close to him. The air here is cold and he begins to feel uneasy.

He forces himself to speak. 'I haven't noticed that, Pete. Everyone seems pretty keyed up.'

Pete is shaking his head. 'Not true, not true.'

John hears a cutlery drawer being opened, the silverware inside rattling slightly. It's going on behind his back, because Pete has him pressed against the counter, waving the whisky bottle in his face. He asks, 'What's going on?'

Pete says, 'Did you see me on the phone when you turned up?'

It was true Pete had a mobile jammed against his ear when he'd opened the front door. John didn't think anything of it at the time—Pete was always on the phone, managing his interests.

'Yeah—who was it?'

Pete nods. 'It was Charlie. He'd been nabbed at the docks. They were waiting for him when the ship come in.'

'What ship?'

'You don't have to pretend you didn't know, John. The Madrigal. Come all the way from South Africa with a little present for us. We paid a lot of money for a bag of uncut diamonds, and guess what? It's all gone to shit. I wonder how that happened?'

Pete's face is up close to his own now. He can see the open pores on Pete's skin, the red blotches on his neck where he hasn't shaved properly, the pale blond hairs of his eyebrows that aren't visible from more than three feet.

'Wasn't me, Pete, honest! I never knew anything about it. Jimmy never said and you haven't said anything. You know you haven't.'

'Flaky, John, flaky. You're just too flaky.'

He begins to panic and reaches behind to put his glass on the counter. Pete has him crushed in a corner, the black granite counter pressing into the small of his back.

Pete says, 'And another thing.'

'What, Pete, what? You're scaring me.'

'I understand we've got you to blame for bringing Dyke and his young 'un into this to begin with. That right?'

Thinking quickly, he tries to work out what Pete means. Then he remembers and his stomach flip-flops. 'Yeah,' he says, lowering his head. 'I told Dan his girlfriend had been seen up here.'

'That's my boy.'

'I didn't know, Pete! I was just doing a favour for a mate. I didn't know Jimmy had got her till afterwards. Just a horrible coincidence, like. Me knowing both of them.'

Pete's shaking his head now. 'Coincidence. More like bad luck, Chief.'

'I don't know what you mean,' he says, trying to control his voice, acting as if this was all nonsense. 'It's what I do — just get to know people. Keep people in touch. I got a knack for it. And I just did what you asked me to, didn't I? Kept you in touch with what Dyke was doing. I didn't do wrong, did I?'

Pete shakes his head again. 'No, you've been a good boy. As far as that's concerned. The problem is, Chief, you talk too much. I don't know who you've been talking to, and I've got tired of worrying about it. You know too much and you do too little.'

'I can do more, Pete!'

'I don't think so, John, I don't think so.'

His voice is teary now and he knows he's nearly close to crying. 'I didn't know, Pete. I didn't know anything about the ship or the diamonds. I wouldn't have said anything to anybody anyway.'

'Trouble is, I can't trust you. I know you too well. Funny – I hardly know Charlie at all but he's the only one I can trust. And he's been fucked over. So what am I supposed to do?'

'Pete, this isn't like you. Everyone knows Jimmy's a nutter but you're the one keeps him in check. This is wrong.'

Pete smiles and John's blood seems to chill.

'I let him run around with his snippers,' Pete says. 'Like a big kid with a toy gun. But behind every hard man there's an even harder man. He knows who's boss. I just have to prove it now and then. This is one of them times, Chief.'

He feels a coldness suddenly across his midriff, and looking down he sees a knife handle sticking out from his stomach. Pete is holding it against him and slowly pushing it in. John feels the coldness spreading — and then the pain thumps him like a closed fist in the gut. He gasps and doubles over but Pete catches him and lowers him slowly to the ground.

He's aware of his cheek against the tiles, now, and there's a strange smell which he thinks might be the odour of his blood as it flows from his stomach. Pete is still speaking but he can't hear. All his concentration is focused on holding back the pain. Steeling himself for when it gets worse. He's sure it will get worse because he's not dead yet. He wonders whether he'll recover from this or whether he's about to die. He doesn't want to die but just at the moment he doesn't have the energy to fight, to crawl, to get away.

He realises that his eyes are closed when he hears the sound of another pair of feet on the tiles. He blinks opens and sees a woman's legs. It must be Marie. He's sorry that she has to see him in this state but it wasn't his fault. Perhaps she'll excuse him. Not hold it against him.

Now she's talking to Pete—more than talking, she's shouting at him. Screaming at him. Pedlar John can hear the shape and the noise of the words but he can't understand them. He can't understand anything any more. It's all noise and movement and the sensation of air on his cheek. He's swimming into a warm sea and all he has left are the thoughts going through his head. He thinks about Marie shouting at Pete because of the mess, and how could he be so stupid, and what are they going to do now. And he thinks of how much feeling she must have inside her. Feeling for Pete and all the time they've had together.

And he thinks, I wonder if that's what people mean when they talk about love.

CHAPTER FORTY-EIGHT

I had no idea why I was driving back to Pete Wilder's house. Perhaps I missed him. Perhaps I wanted to make sure I knew where he was. Perhaps there was unfinished business between us. Or perhaps I thought I'd find Jimmy there.

As I parked in the road opposite the entrance to Pete's house the iron gates between the poplars opened and Marie Wilder drove out in a white Mercedes CLK with the top down. As she paused to turn into the road she saw me. She stared hard at me then looked away and drove off. I climbed out of my car and crossed the road. Walking through the entrance I saw that Pete's front door was still open—Marie must have left in a hurry. All the lights in the house were on. The Wilders weren't fussy about using electricity; they wanted to see everything that was happening around them.

I waited outside and listened. There was no sound coming from the house. Not even a television programme or music. No chatter between Pete and Jimmy, though I doubted that Jimmy was here because his Corvette wasn't to be seen. I hesitated because I didn't have a weapon. I'd come to talk to Pete, I realised, not to fight him.

I stepped inside the door onto the hard tiles. I remembered where his living room was and stepped towards it.

Then felt an arm around my neck and a knife pricking my right kidney.

'Walk very, very slowly,' Pete said, and let me go with his left arm.

The knife remained pressed into my back.

He pointed me towards his games room, straight ahead, and we walked in. He told me to stop for a moment. I heard a drawer open in a cupboard, then the knife was withdrawn from my back. It was replaced by the cold metal of a gun barrel against the nape of my neck.

'You know what this is, Chief?'

'A blow-pipe?' I said.

'Ha ha. Walk over to the black chair and sit down.'

The last time I'd been in this room was during daylight hours. Now it was dark outside each of the electronic gadgets gave off a small coloured nimbus—green, blue, red. Black box piled on black box, each with its own lighting eco-system. It was like a set from Blade Runner built for ants.

'I thought Jimmy was the big kid,' I said. 'But you like shiny stuff too.'

'Don't start,' he said. I was sitting facing him now while he'd remained standing. He wore his usual white tee-shirt and black jeans, and was pointing a small pistol at me. It looked like a Walther. He took a deep breath and seemed to calm himself. 'So what do you want, Chief?' he asked. 'Come to crack a few more jokes at my expense?'

'I warned you once about messing with my family.'

'So?'

'You didn't listen, did you?'

'You're not making any sense, Chief. What have I done to you?'

'It's more like what you haven't done.'

He shifted his weight. 'What's that supposed to mean?'

'You've been using Jimmy like a blunt weapon to intimidate the people around me.'

'You're crackers.'

'I didn't get it at first. I thought Jimmy was just unmanageable. But then I realised that you were the smart one. You were the one actually pulling the strings.'

'Whatever my brother's done, that's his lookout. In case you hadn't noticed, he's a grown man.'

'He's got a grown man's muscles, I'll grant you that.'

Pete's face grew darker. 'I've had enough of this shit for one night. Stand up.'

I looked at him until he took a step towards me, then I slowly stood up.

'Turn around and put your hands behind you.'

I turned to look out of the back windows, into his illuminated garden. It was lit up like Las Vegas in hues of green, blue and red. He'd replicated outside the colour palette of his electronic kit inside. I waited for the blow to the back of my head. But it didn't come.

Instead he grabbed one of my arms and pushed it up my back, then manoeuvred me so that I was walking ahead of him. We walked out of the living room and turned left into the kitchen. I smelled a strong odour of lemon soap but the first thing I saw was Pedlar John, sprawled out on the floor with a pool of blood still oozing from his midriff.

Pete saw me looking. 'Forgot to take out the rubbish,' he said. 'Stand there.'

Behind my back he opened a drawer and felt around. I could see us both reflected in the dark windows and I saw that his eyes never left the back of my head despite the fact that he was searching for something with his free hand. He seemed to find it.

'Okay, back in the front room,' he said, and we returned the way we'd come. I wondered how long Pedlar John had been lying there.

'Did Marie like you messing up her kitchen?' I asked.

He ignored me. 'Sit down again. Tie yourself to the chair.'

I sat down in his black swivel chair and he threw a clothes-line into my lap. I laid my left hand on top of the arm of the chair and wrapped the line around it and under the arm, then crossed it over to the other side.

'Can't tie it off,' I told him.

He squatted beside me and seized my arm with his strong left, then laid his gun on the floor, grabbed the line and wrapped it around my right wrist several times, strapping it to the arm. Then he took the spare line and wrapped it around my feet so that I couldn't stand. Finally he knotted the line, picked up his gun and stood. I felt my heart begin to thump a little faster.

'Not so sharp now,' Pete said. 'But I think you've got more to learn.'

'What do you mean?'

'Wait here,' he said. 'Oh, you've got no choice, have you?'

He turned and left the room. He was gone about thirty seconds and when he came back he held a pair of secateurs in his left hand, mirroring the pistol he still held in his right. He had suddenly become a slimmer version of his own brother—less bulk, less obvious madness, but perhaps equally obsessive.

'Is it all unravelling?' I said. 'You've suddenly lost control of your brother, who's not doing what you want any more. The diamonds have gone west. There's no way in hell you're going to develop the Dorset Estate now. And Marie's done a runner too.'

He took a step forward. 'Will you stop talking about Marie?' he shouted. 'Leave her out of it.'

'What, like you did, killing a defenceless boy in her kitchen? Did she see it? Is that why she left? I saw her go, Pete. I don't think she's coming back.'

'I warned you,' he said, and came closer. He dropped the Walther on the sofa behind him and came to stand right in front of me. 'Jimmy nearly did you, didn't he? Well I'm going to finish you off. After a little lesson.'

I'd made a fist of my right hand but he easily pried my fingers apart. I could smell the sweat on his body and saw the bumps and ridges on the top of his head through his cropped hair. I struggled to get my left hand free but I'd wrapped the line too tight.

'You don't want this, Pete,' I gasped. 'This isn't you. You're the one with the brains.'

'Keep talking, Chief, I'll snip your tongue off too.'

'Jimmy does it because he can't help himself. It's the only way he has of being a man. You're different.'

He had my fingers splayed on top of the arm and was working the secateurs towards them. I tried to swivel the chair but he was so heavy I couldn't move it.

I started to talk again but he interrupted. 'People never do what you want, do they?' he asked. He had the secateurs around my right forefinger. 'You come up with a perfectly good plan and they fuck it up.'

'Don't do this, Pete. It's not worth it.'

'Not for you, maybe.'

'It makes you both the same. And you're not. You're better than him.'

This thought seemed to hit him. He hesitated and his grip

loosened.

'Just because you're twins doesn't mean you're the same. You can think. You don't have to bully like him. You've got the same genes but you're different inside. You've got family. You've got a wife. Someone who wants to see you safe.'

'I told you ... '

'Marie doesn't want you to come to harm, does she? She doesn't like it when you're in danger. Jimmy doesn't have that. It's why he kidnapped Kelly, to try to get what you've got. But it didn't work.'

'Will you quit talking about that girl! He let her out ages ago.'

'Is that what he told you?'

'What do you mean?'

'He kept hold of her, Pete. Just two days ago he took her to that place you have. That safe house.'

He was shaking his head, not wanting to believe me.

I realised something. 'You told him to release her, didn't you? You knew it would make things worse for both of you. For Christ's sake – you think he's listening to you now? He's gone way too far down the line.'

All the air suddenly left him, as though I'd been struggling with a life-sized blow-up doll that was suddenly deflated. He sagged and fell back on his haunches.

'That stupid bastard,' he said. 'That big, dumb, stupid bastard.'

I said nothing for half a minute while Pete got his bearings. He stared at the floor as if it might contain the answers that would make everything right again.

'I thought it would work out,' he said. 'I thought he'd see sense, come round. I always do.' He let out a short laugh, then looked up at me, his eyes hard. 'All your fucking fault, ain't it? And that stupid girl. He could never let anything go. Fucking obsessed, he was.'

'Untie me, Pete,' I said.

He didn't move. Then he said, 'I've got to think about this, Chief. What to do. I don't know what to do.'

'Untie me and we'll sort it out.'

'Wait!' he said. 'Let me think.'

Then another voice said, 'Yeah, think Pete. That's what you do. Unlike the big, dumb, stupid bastard who happens to be your brother.'

Little Jimmy walked into the room, his size and his manner demonstrating yet again the extreme irony of his nickname. He hadn't changed. He was wearing the same clothes he wore when I'd fought him at Laura's house. He still carried the machete in his right arm and the blood from the candlestick wounds had dried on his black tee-shirt. Pete stood up and faced him.

'Where the fuck have you been?' he asked.

'Sorting someone out,' Jimmy said. 'Him, as a matter of fact.'

'Yeah, he looks sorted, doesn't he?'

Pete turned around, bent down and started snipping the clothesline around my wrists. Jimmy shouted at him.

'What are you doing? Leave the fucker be.'

Pete ignored him. 'It's finished, Jimmy. It's too late. We can't go back.'

'I said leave him!'

Jimmy stepped up behind his brother and smashed him with the handle of the machete. Pete groaned and tipped to one side, then fell heavily to the floor. My right hand was free and I was unravelling the left as Jimmy stood to his full height in front of me.

'Think the odds are about right?' I asked him.

'Run away now, fuck face,' he said taking another step forward, swinging the machete casually.

'Okay.'

The last coil of the rope had come away from my wrist. As it did, the rope loosened and fell from my ankles, too. I pushed and swivelled the chair away just as Jimmy lunged at me. I felt his machete thud into the top of the chair as I rolled off it, and kept rolling towards the back door.

'No place to go, Sammy.'

'Only my best friends call me that,' I said. 'You don't qualify.'

I was upright now and grabbing the handle of the glass door. It opened and I ran outside, hearing Jimmy thundering behind me. Big isn't necessarily fast, but he had a long reach with the knife so I kept running into the illuminated garden. It was like wandering into a toytown Las Vegas. My clothes changed colour as I was caught by the different coloured lights Pete had directed towards his statues and garden furniture.

I ran across the lawn towards the shadows at the bottom of the garden. Then I stopped and turned around. It had gone quiet except for the twittering of a couple of birds in a nearby garden. Jimmy had stepped back inside. I saw his silhouette moving about inside the games room. I looked around, getting my bearings, feeling the sweat cool on my shirt. I could smell the evening exhalations from the flowers and shrubs around me. Pete's statues were scattered about on the lawn and set into the flower beds, each lit from below. To my right was a swing chair and to my left was the garden pavilion with its gabled roof and banister, looking like a small Tyrolean chalet that had got lost.

I crouched low and ran until I could stand behind the

pavilion's rear corner. As I watched the back of the house Jimmy reappeared again, this time without the machete but with his brother's gun. He stood in the doorway silhouetted by the house lights behind him.

'I didn't even know you were here!' he shouted in my general direction. 'Come to talk to my brother and what do I find? Bonus! So let's you and me talk, Sammy.' He waited, shifting from foot to foot. I didn't move.

He said, 'Okay, let's play,' and stepped out of the house. He raised the gun and fired in my general direction. The bullet crashed through the trees at my back. Then I saw him running more or less straight towards me, like a bull with one intent—kill the matador.

I shifted my weight so I was directly behind the pavilion and listened to his heavy steps over the grass. They stopped and I extended my hearing into the darkness to find him. He wasn't even breathing hard.

I felt a sudden searing pain in my right shoulder before I heard the gun shot. A bullet had hit me from behind. Its impact tumbled me forward, away from the pavilion and into a flower bed. Jimmy had skirted the other end of the pavilion and seen me before I'd sensed him.

'Yes!' he shouted. 'He shoots, he scores.'

I kept moving, scrabbling to my knees and getting upright. I turned back towards the house and ran, holding my shoulder with my other hand.

I heard Jimmy forcing his way through the undergrowth until he was rounding the end of the pavilion and chasing me again. The rear door of the house was ahead of me, light spilling from it on to Pete's extensive patio. I kept it framed in my eye-line as I sped towards it.

Then the light was blocked by a figure. It stood in the doorway, weaving slightly.

Pete had recovered enough to stand.

I let out a swear word but kept going. Perhaps I had enough momentum to barrel him aside and force my way past, then out of the front door to my car.

'Pete!' Jimmy called from behind me. 'Stop him!'

As I drew close I saw an expression on Pete's face that I couldn't read. It was half in shadow but the enigma went deeper than that. There was a kind of resignation mixed with sadness in the set of his mouth.

I sped towards him, ready to turn my shoulder into his chest. But at the last moment he stepped aside and I flew past him into the house. I crashed to a halt against the back of a chair and turned around, pain tearing through my upper chest. Pete had resumed his position in the doorway, facing Jimmy's approach. I heard two dull shots from outside and the glass door shattered. Pete turned sideways to look at the falling glass just as Jimmy came thundering in.

I saw the flash of the machete before I realised what Pete was doing. He had raised it to shoulder-height.

'No, Pete!' I shouted.

He ignored me. And as Jimmy ran past him, Pete slashed the machete horizontally across his brother's throat.

Jimmy paused, half-turned and raised his free hand to his neck. Then he looked down at it, at the blood that soaked his fingers and was now flowing freely down the front of his black tee-shirt. He stumbled and Pete caught him, holding him close to his chest.

'What you done, Pete? What was that for?'

'You were right, Jimmy. I was the dumb, stupid bastard, not you. It's for the best. Now lie still.'

Holding Jimmy under the arms, Pete moved slowly to the floor and I saw that he had a bullet wound above his collar bone, at the base of his neck, and was bleeding profusely.

One of the last two shots must have been aimed at him. The brothers sank as ponderously as prehistoric creatures caught on film.

I went to my knees and watched the slow ballet as they fell. They were oblivious to me now.

Jimmy tried to speak again but his destroyed throat made it impossible. His arms flailed and the gun arced away from him. Pete pulled him up and held him tight, his eyes glassy and moist. Their heads almost touched, as though they were communing.

At last, after an age, the twins fell silently on to the carpeted floor, where the last exertions of their failing hearts pumped out blood that flowed and mingled and entwined them both, soaking their clothes and at last transforming the black and white that had made them distinct from each other into a single scarlet.

And that was the moment that Moody and his men came crashing through the front door in a racket of yelling, clod-hopping, leather-clad stupidity.

Moody came into the room and looked down at me.

'A day late and a dollar short,' I said.

And after that I didn't feel much like talking.

CHAPTER FORTY-NINE

Laura had driven to the hospital to pick me up. She brought Dan with her. He sat in the back seat staring silently out of the windows while Laura drove me home. Both my arms had been dealt with and they now hurt like hell. Fortunately the bullet had only gone through my upper right arm, not my shoulder as I'd thought.

'How did Moody know about the diamonds?' Laura asked. I'd told her some of the background while waiting for the doctor to look at me. 'The twins were under surveillance all this time?'

'From the beginning. Their contact in South Africa was nabbed after he put the diamonds on the ship. He gave the twins up straight away. They were amateurs playing in the wrong park.'

'So when the ship docked the police arrested the Wilders' men? That simple?

'More or less. The container was unloaded and whoever went in first was it. That happened to be Pete's man, Charlie.'

'So where was Moody when you wanted him?'

'Getting ready to raid the wrong house,' I said. 'The twins only lived two streets apart so they didn't think it was worthwhile having units outside both. Jimmy was usually the more active of the two, so they watched his place.'

'But didn't he go home after attacking us? Didn't they pick him up there?'

'Apparently not. He hadn't changed when he barged in on Pete and me. Perhaps he went for a curry first.'

Dan snorted in the back seat. I turned to look at him but he avoided my eyes.

'I half expected to see you come roaring out of the garden shed, kick-boxing the statues to smithereens.'

Laura said, 'Leave him alone, Sam.'

I turned back. I supposed she was right. Dan had come up to the North West to find Kelly. He'd done that and had virtually no thanks for it. And now she had been taken from him again. I'd forgotten how bitter young love could be.

We drove in silence down the motorway. It was after midnight and the traffic was just about manageable, the occasional glare of headlights swooping past us as a boy-racer swept off on his way south.

'Thanks for fetching me,' I said.

'I'm getting used to it.'

'The police have taken my car.'

'Just another hassle, isn't it?'

I looked sideways at her.

'Are we OK?' I asked.

She shrugged. 'You mean after having been attacked by a psychopath with a machete, questioned by the police for two hours, being abandoned by you while you go off to get shot at, being called out in the dead of night with my neck still showing machete rash ... All right, I suppose you could say I'm not happy. Happiness is not on my radar at the moment.

Happiness is a dark galaxy, far, far away.'

'I'm sorry. Things happen.'

'No, Sam, things don't just happen. You make them happen. You got caught up and wound up and in the end you just had a vendetta against these ... these thugs. You nearly got both of us killed.'

'But we're alive and they're both dead.'

'Oh, so that's OK then.'

Dan said, 'Will you two stop it?' He paused, then added, 'I'm going back to London tomorrow. I've got nothing to stay up here for.'

Now Laura looked sideways at me. We'd discussed this earlier, while we'd been waiting for the police at her house.

I cleared my throat. 'You don't have to go to London,' I said. 'We—I—would like you to stay up here. With us.'

'What, so I can referee?'

'Don't be like that, Dan,' Laura said. 'This isn't exactly a typical night out.'

'And I've been thinking,' I said.

'There's a first time for everything I suppose.'

'I can't make any promises,' I said. 'But you've shown some guts in the last couple of weeks. I was thinking I might start a detecting dynasty. What do you think?'

He leaned forward. 'What, you mean like working with you? You laughed last time I mentioned it.'

'I laugh at lots of things,' I said. 'It's the sixth law of private detection. Never take anything too seriously. If you did, you might cry.'

'Then where would you be?' Laura asked, enigmatically.

I said nothing.

Other Works

The Sam Dyke Series

Altered Life
The Private Lie
The Hard Swim
The Bleak
The Strange Girl
The Secret Sharers
The Innocent Dead
The Lonely Grave
The Second Guess (short story)

Paul Storey Thrillers

Storey
One Punch
The Song of Geneva Chance

Standalone Novels

A French Darcy – a Romance
Actress – a Contemporary novel

Essays on Writing

The Idle Writer
Crime Writing Confidential

Blog

www.cwconfidential.blogspot.com

Webpage

http://www.keithdixonnovels.com

www.ingramcontent.com/pod-product-compliance
Lightning Source LLC
Chambersburg PA
CBHW020134310726
48970CB00006B/1870